Quest

Fulton River Falls: Book Five

Diana Rock

Also by Diana Rock

Colby County Series
Bid To Love
Courting Choices

Fulton River Falls
Melt My Heart
Proof of Love
Bloomin' In Love
First Christmas Ornament: A Fulton River Falls Novella
Quest For Love

MovieStuds
Hollywood Hotshot

Standalone
Little Bit of Wait
Havilland's Highland Destiny: A Contemporary Highland Romance

Watch for more at DianaRock.com.

Trigger Warning: Memories of child sexual assault

Copyright 2024 © by Denise M. Long
All Rights reserved.
No part of this book may be used or
reproduced in any manner whatsoever
including audio recording or AI without written
permission of the author and Copyright holder.
This author supports the right to free expression and
values copyright protection.
The scanning, uploading, and distribution of
this book in any manner or medium
without permission of the copyright holder
is theft of the property.
Thank you for supporting this author's
creative work with your purchase.

FIRST EDITION
Digital ISBN: 9798986757186
Paperback ISBN: 9798986757193

Editor: Lynne Pearson, All that Editing

This is a work of fiction. Names, characters, places, and incidents either are the product of the author's imagination or are used fictitiously, and any resemblance to actual persons, living or dead, business establishments, organizations, events, or locale, is entirely coincidental.

CHAPTER ONE

"The alterations fee comes to six hundred fifty-eight dollars."

Caroline handed over her MasterCard and watched as the woman swiped the card. The woman blinked several times after a quiet beep emitted from the POS machine. "It's declined," she whispered, holding out the card.

The garment bag with her altered fifteen thousand dollar gala ballgown dangled from Caroline's left index finger. She glared at the shop owner. "What do you mean it was declined?" Her pinched voice squeaked like a mouse caught by its tail in a trap. "Try it again. I need this gown!"

The flustered woman stared back, fear accentuating her eyes like a deer in the headlights as she held out the card in a trembling hand. Her pupils dilated even more as Caroline snatched it back. "I'm sorry. Perhaps you have another?" Her voice trembled as she clasped and unclasped her hands on the checkout counter.

Her eyes shooting daggers, Caroline set the garment bag back on the hanger. She rummaged through her wallet to pull out every one of her credit cards. Slapping the stack down on the counter, she glared at the shop woman and threw back her shoulders defiantly. "Try them. Try them all if you must. I don't understand why it's being declined. You must be doing something wrong."

The saleswoman spread them out, separating her store credit cards, Saks, Nordstrom, Bergdorf Goodman, Hermès, Gucci, Chanel, Ferragamo, Louis Vuitton, Dolce & Gabbana, Michael Kors, and Dior from the American Express, Visa, another MasterCard, and a Discover card.

Under Caroline's scrutiny, the woman tried every major credit card she had before her. Caroline's blood pressure escalated with each beep. Heat built under her Michael Kors leather jacket. This clumsy situation was making her perspire all over the Chanel dress she'd bought yesterday with the same card.

After the last of the cards was rejected, the woman gingerly slid them back across the counter with the tip of her index finger. "Apple Pay or Google Pay? Venmo? PayPal?"

Caroline swiped the POS terminal on the counter with her cellphone. Her scowl grew darker and darker with each decline. The shop owner cringed with each flat tone.

When all her options had failed, Caroline's face turned from red hot to pale white as she and the saleswoman stared at each other across the counter.

"Cash?" asked the saleswoman, her voice barely a whisper. But it was too late. The commotion at the checkout desk had become apparent to the other shoppers and sales staff in the Fifth Avenue couture boutique.

The whispering in the background accelerated as Caroline shook her head slightly. Her mind spun. Her words were sharp as she replied through clenched teeth, "I don't carry seven hundred dollars in cash around with me when I go shopping." She pulled out her checkbook. "How about a check?"

As if hissed at by an asp, the woman stepped back from the counter. "No. We don't accept personal checks."

Caroline's gaze flicked away to the women witnessing her humiliating treatment. Glaring back at the saleswoman, she used her free hand to sweep the pile of declined credit cards into her open purse. "Great."

For a few seconds, she stood stock still in silence. The audience surrounding her seemed to hold its breath, waiting for someone to make the next move. She darted a glance at the bag. "I paid for the dress already."

Abruptly, Caroline reached for the garment bag as the woman tried to snatch it off the hanger. Anger flared so strongly that Caroline was afraid her head would explode. "It's still mine." Her voice deep and threatening, she held firmly to the bag with her right hand.

"Not until you pay for the alterations you demanded," The saleswoman said firmly, her gaze sweeping the assembled crowd.

Caroline turned and took a step toward the door with the dress bag held aloft. The saleswoman called out, "If you step one foot outside that door, I will be forced to call the police."

Caroline froze but didn't turn back. The last thing she needed was to be carted down to the police station. If someone made the connection to her father, it would become all the more embarrassing. There had to be some simple misunderstanding. A phone call to her accountant, Henry DuBois, would fix it. He always fixed everything. She was not going to miss the gala ball. "I will be back for it after I call my accountant."

"We close in twenty-two minutes. And we are closed tomorrow."

Caroline couldn't breathe. If she left with the dress, she would be charged with theft. But if she left without it, she wouldn't have anything to where to the Met Gala.

Held high above her head, she flipped her right hand palm down, letting the bag with the one-of-a-kind, custom-fitted, and altered Ellie Sabb couture ballgown drop to the floor in a heap. Gasps from onlookers filled the quiet space as Caroline pivoted in her Manolo heels and marched out the shop door.

Out on the sidewalk, she stood squinting in the early May sunshine. Her face was hot, her insides roiling like a tea kettle left on a burner for too long. Her hand searched her jacket pocket, pulling out her Dior sunglasses. The over-bright afternoon sunshine made her head ache even more. Her armpits were damp, a revolting consequence of her problem.

Clearly, the saleswoman didn't have a clue what she was doing with the credit card machine. Whatever the cause, Caroline was sure the accountant could fix the problem. Then, she would fire him for letting such a humiliating episode happen.

She dove her hand into her MK purse in search of her phone. A swarm of credit cards erupted in a shower of plastic to scatter around her feet.

A young man passing by stooped to pick them up for her. He jumped back as Caroline snarled, "Get away. Those useless cards are mine."

The man's face darkened as he retreated. With a scowl, he barked back, "Suit yourself. I was only trying to help." And he strode off.

Dropping to squat as best she could in her thigh-high boots, she pulled the cards into a pile and threw them back in her purse. Standing, she noticed the crowd inside the boutique was intently watching her predicament through the shop window. Caroline strode off, going as far as the next intersection before turning the corner and pulling out her phone.

She punched the contact button for her accountant and waited as the phone rang in his Fulton River, Vermont office.

When a woman's voice answered, "DuBois and Son," Caroline grimaced as she cradled the phone to her ear. "This is Caroline Perret. I need to speak with Henry immediately."

"One moment, please."

The line clicked over, and a male voice answered, "Michael DuBois speaking. How can I help you?"

Caroline's insides seethed. "I asked for Henry. This is Caroline Perret. Put him on the phone, I need to speak with him immediately."

"Ms. Perret, this is Michael DuBois, his son. We've been trying to reach you for months."

"I'm having an emergency. I must speak to Henry immediately." Heat blossomed in her chest, the pressure escalating to a boiling point yet again. "I don't care what you want. You need to fix *my* problem. *All* of my credit cards have been declined. Even Apple, Venmo, and Google

QUEST FOR LOVE

Pay have declined my last purchase attempt. You must fix the problem immediately."

The voice on the phone hardened. "Ms. Perret, your credit card accounts have been frozen. Your failure to respond to our emails, letters, and voice messages forced my hand. All our unanswered attempts over the last three months have left me with no other option."

Caroline remembered deleting a bunch of emails and voice messages on her cell phone from the accountant's office over the last months. All without reading them or listening to them. "Frozen? Unfreeze them immediately. I must pay for the gown I'm wearing to the Met Gala tomorrow evening."

"I'm sorry, Ms. Perret. My fiduciary responsibility means I can't do that. I can explain the situation if you could come to our office tomorrow morning."

Her hands trembling, Caroline asked, "What situation? I'm in Manhattan. I need to check in to my hotel room at the Ritz. I don't have time to return to Vermont. Can't you tell me over the phone?"

"Your room reservation was canceled." His voice turned impatient. "I can't stress strongly enough the need to speak with you. In person."

Ignoring the quivering in her stomach, Caroline's spine went rigid as her shoulders thrust back. "Canceled? You canceled my room block for the weekend? My friends and I are staying there."

"I'm sorry, but it had to be done. There's a circumstance that desperately needs your attention."

"Stop dithering. Tell me what's wrong now, or I'll find myself another accounting firm."

The phone line was silent for a few seconds as if he were debating the options. Then Mr. DuBois took a deep breath and sighed. "Ms. Perret, you're broke."

CHAPTER TWO

It was a long tiresome trip back to Montpelier in her chauffeur-driven Lincoln town car, fortunately paid for in advance. As she sat in the cushy, black leather-covered back seat, she examined her finger nails, now in need of a manicure. She didn't know if she would be able to keep her appointment for her facial, massage, manicure, and pedicure at the hotel tomorrow morning. Could she possibly get back to New York City in time for the gala? Did she have anything appropriate to wear? It was unthinkable to show up in what she wore last year. She would rather not go than suffer the humiliation of wearing the same ball gown twice.

The driver pulled up at her lovely brownstone townhouse. He carried her suitcases all the way upstairs to her bedroom, laying them on her king-sized, satin-covered bed before departing. "What time should I pick you up tomorrow morning, madam?"

Caroline chewed her lower lip for a second. "I'll let you know tomorrow. Thank you." If she were able to straighten out this mess and find something to wear, she might be able to get back to the city in time for the gala's red carpet.

The chauffeur nodded and left.

Caroline sat on the edge of her bed and flopped onto her back, thinking about the $250,000 she'd paid to reserve her table. They didn't just let anyone attend the event. The organizers had balked at her attempt to get one. In the end, she had to mention her father, the Vermont senator to the US Congress. They weren't thrilled, but after reviewing the list of people who would be seated at the table with her, they agreed. Her seven friends not only had instant celebrity recognition as New England society icons and social media influencers but also very deep pockets. The organizers likely hoped the fresh, eager socialites would donate to the institute. But it was all for naught.

QUEST FOR LOVE

She would meet her accountant and ream him out for letting the situation get so bad.

Seated in front of Henry DuBois's desk the next morning, Caroline waited. She fidgeted in her seat, first tugging at one sleeve of her couture daywear, then the mini skirt that slid up her thighs too far. Gnawing at her bottom lip, she couldn't remember how she managed to get to here.

A kind, male voice sounded behind her as she heard the office door open and close. "I'm sorry to keep you waiting, Ms. Perret." The tall, trim, ash-blond man in a well-fitting but tired-looking navy business suit shook her hand before settling behind the desk. "We have a lot of things to discuss," he said, sliding a pile of folders into the center of his desk.

A tremor ran through her. "Wait. Who are you? And where's Henry?"

His face took on a grim, pinched look. "I'm Henry's son, Michael." The man sat back in his chair. "My father died over two months ago. I'm managing the business now."

Her mouth opened, ready with a curt retort, but she stopped her tongue. She had not expected that answer. "I'm—I'm sorry for your loss. I didn't know." Embarrassment blossomed in her chest at failing to send a sympathy card or flowers. "He was a good man."

Michael nodded, then shifted his head slightly. "It was rather sudden."

"Is your family okay? Your mom? Don't you have younger siblings?"

Michael nodded again. "Yeah. I'm taking care of Mom, my sister, Pamela, and my two younger brothers, Alan, who will graduate high school in another month, and Jason, who's sixteen."

She didn't know what else to say. Silence settled over the office space.

He broke it by changing the subject. "I have been trying to contact you for months now. Since my father first became ill."

Caroline thought of all the voice messages from the accounting firm she'd deleted. All the letters she had unceremoniously pitched into the garbage can without opening them. "I wasn't aware there was such an urgent problem."

He sighed deeply. "Did you listen to the messages, read the emails or letters? Did you even open them?"

A hot blush raced up her neck to her cheeks. "No," she whispered.

He opened the folder and glanced down, a light flush staining his high cheekbones. "I will try to explain as best as I can." He held out a single page across his desk.

Taking the page, Caroline stared down at it, trying to figure out what it was. She might have graduated from Smith, but accounting had not been her major. In fact, partying was the only major she would have excelled in.

"It's a balance sheet, Ms. Perret." He pointed with his pencil to each section as he explained, "It summarizes all your assets, your liabilities, and your net worth. Or, as the case may be, your net loss."

A glance down at the bottom line before Caroline's eyes flew back to Mr. DuBois's. "This can't be right. I have three million dollars from my grandmother's legacy in my account." A funny flip in her stomach made her sit up straighter.

"No, Ms. Perret. You once had three million dollars. Right now, your net worth is nearly zero."

Her mouth opened to speak, but no words came out. "Where did it go? Are you sure? Did someone abscond with my money?" Her vision blurred as she looked from the page to Mr. DuBois and back again.

He rocked back and forth in his chair, the blush in his cheekbones rising again. "You spent it."

Her throat thickened, preventing her from saying anything beyond a gasp. She stood and began to pace the small office. "How could

I spend three million dollars? I just got it last year." Her bare legs wobbled as she forced them to carry her back and forth in the office.

Blank-faced, the accountant watched her pace to the window and back to the desk. "Clothes and jewels. Your chartered cruise to Monte Carlo with fifty of your closest friends. Your luxury townhouse here in Montpelier. And all the gifts and parties you threw."

"But—" She pressed her palm to her forehead as her mind swirled with all he was saying. "But I could afford it all. He said—" And a flood of memories came back to her. Henry's warnings, his insistence that she lay off the credit cards, stop buying cars for her girlfriends, stop flying the troupe of them around the world for this party or that event. He even tried to talk her out of the townhouse, but she had insisted.

Michael closed his eyes and nodded, trying to ignore her incredible legs almost fully exposed by her miniskirt. He rocked gently in his desk chair. When he opened his eyes, he saw the dismay flutter across her porcelain features. Her sleek, blonde hair shone as rays of sunlight glimmered through the window, landing on her as she walked through their path. With each moment, each step, his pants got a little tighter. He'd have to stay seated until his erection subsided. If it ever subsided. *How can it with her prancing around my office?* He concentrated on watching the weight of his news settle on her slim shoulders. Shoulders that fell lower and lower as she walked in silence around the room.

Her palm still pressed to her forehead, her pacing slowed until she stopped before his desk. "Now what? Bankruptcy?"

Michael gestured toward the chair she'd vacated. "Please sit down."

When she had settled back into her chair, he continued, "I set aside a very small buffer of money. Twenty thousand dollars. It's not enough, but it can keep you financially solvent until you can rectify the situation."

Caroline blinked rapidly several times before asking, "How can I rectify the situation?"

"I suggest an austerity plan. You will have to downsize and—"

"Downsize?" she interrupted. "How can I downsize?"

"You currently have five cars, three of which require monthly payments. I suggest you keep one of the five. Preferably one you actually own. It will lower your insurance premium, your garaging costs, and, of course, your car payments." He paused before adding, "You might even make some money unless you short-sell."

"One? Keep only one?" Her eyes were wide with surprise. "I have to choose?"

"Yes. Keep the most practical. I suggest you sell the Hummer and the Jaguar, get rid of the Mustang and the Astin Martin. Keep the Range Rover. It's the most suitable for Vermont winters."

"No!" She jumped up and resumed her pacing. "I love my Mustang. It was a present. I won't sell it."

"That's not all," he interjected. When she turned to look at him, he continued. "You should sell the townhouse before they foreclose."

"Foreclose!" Her eyes widened even more. "It's my home."

He stood to face her, and leaned on his hands on his desk top. He hoped the tenting in his trousers wasn't noticeable. "Ms. Perret. You are in a desperate situation. You have to cut back. Way back." He nodded in response to the shaking of her head in disagreement. "Yes." He opened his mouth to say something and then thought better of it. After a few seconds, he added. "And you must find a job."

She reached toward the desk as though she were going to faint. He hurried around the desk and grasped her elbow to steer her to the chair. She slumped into it and crumpled into a ball, her hands over her face.

From a small dorm-sized refrigerator, he retrieved a bottle of cool water, poured half of it into a highball glass, and handed it to her. "Here, this might help."

QUEST FOR LOVE

Her eyes had a glazed look to them when she raised her head. Still, she grasped the glass and sipped for several minutes. At length, she returned his gaze, the glint in her eyes telling him she had her wits about her once again.

They stared at each other as a clock ticked. Then her eyes lit up.

"I don't have to do all that." She straightened up, her face suddenly brilliant.

He raised an eyebrow. "What do you mean? Have you thought of something else?"

She sat back in her chair, looking like the cat who swallowed the canary. "I have. If you remember the terms of my Grandmother's trust, I got three million dollars when I turned twenty-one. The remainder of the trust money comes to me when I marry."

"That's just it. You'd have to get married to satisfy the stipulations of the trust. And prove it."

Caroline winked as she replied, "I can manage that easily enough. Lots of men would love to marry me." She sat back, a smug look spreading across her delicate features. "Besides, once I have the money, I can get a divorce."

He paused for a few moments, his index fingers steepled in front of his lips. "Don't forget, Vermont is an equitable distribution state. Once you marry, half of that money will likely belong to your spouse. He would keep it in a divorce."

"Shit," Caroline muttered. "But what's left in the trust? Surely it will be more than enough to allow me to keep all my cars and my townhouse."

"Perhaps, if you economize. It won't last forever. You'll need to invest most of it to live off." He paused, hoping the import of his words would change her exorbitant spending habits. "If *that* is your plan, you need to marry within the next four weeks. There just isn't enough money to meet your basic needs longer than that. Especially if you decide to keep everything." He paused again. "Don't forget, it takes a few weeks for the trust fund money to be transferred. It's not automatically available on your wedding day."

Her pensive gaze unsettled him. He glanced away rather than get lost in those beautiful Grecian blue eyes. "At last check, there was nearly ten million dollars left."

"Ten left? A year ago, Henry told me it was up to twelve million. What happened to the money? Where did it all go?"

Michael knew this question was coming. He'd done his homework. "Between the investment choices you selected, the economic downturn and inflation have cut down the worth of your investments. Presuming you inherit today." She could have lived comfortably for years if she had placed even half of it into CDs. Then again, if the woman had bothered to pay attention to any of their attempts to communicate with her, Michael and his father could have restructured her high-risk investments to prevent some of the loss.

"But the longer I hold off on receiving it, the more might come back?"

He sighed. "Potentially, if the market turns. But don't forget, you can't last more than a month on the remains of your savings unless you marry quickly."

CHAPTER THREE

"What about my upcoming trips to Europe with my friends?" At least she still had that to look forward to.

His composure slipped. "In an effort to save your finances, I suggest you cancel the trips. The deposits are nonrefundable, but you won't be responsible for the remaining payments."

Caroline's knees felt weak again. "I have to tell all my girlfriends the trips are off?"

He nodded, his face still impassive.

The gears in her brain whirled, looking for options. Mr. DuBois sat patiently before her, no sign of emotion on his face. A thought bloomed. He looked familiar. The long narrow face, the angular jaw coming to a dimpled chin. Those brilliant green eyes were familiar. They were the same color as his father's. She stirred in her seat. "How long ago was it when we first met?"

He smiled and nodded. "We were both a lot younger. Maybe ten or eleven. My father used to oversee your father's accounts. I believe we met a few times when you came here with him."

"Hmm," she said. "You were the messy-haired blond kid who hid under your father's desk when we came?"

A barely suppressed half-grimace formed on his face. "Yes. I admit it. That was me." His face brightened as if he remembered something important. "I almost forgot." He dug into his desk drawer and pulled out a one-hundred dollar bill. "This is for you. Make it last the entire week."

She gulped as she took it from him. It was a fresh bill, the texture scratchy against her soft hand. "All week? What about food, or gas, or drinks?"

Mr. Dubois glared at her. "One hundred dollars for everything. Spend it very wisely. You won't get any more until a week from today."

Her breathing grew shallow and fast. "But—I need more than that to get through a single day." She flashed him an exasperated look. Mr. Dubois's face remained stony. Since that avenue wasn't working, she batted her eyelashes. "Please, sir. I want some more."

"The Oliver Twist line isn't going to work." He crossed his arms over his chest sternly. "That's all you get. If you need more money than that, you'll have to get a job faster." He opened the desk drawer again and pulled out two business cards. "Here's the real estate agent I suggest you use. Call as soon as possible. You have to get rid of those massive mortgage payments, preferably before the next one is due in a week."

Caroline took the cards from him without saying a word. She didn't trust herself to be nice about the situation. She had to sell her cars. She had to sell her home. She had to give up everything she held dear. She shot him a sour look.

"Don't give me that look. It's long past time you learned the true value of money." He stood and walked around the desk. "That second business card is for the auto dealer interested in buying your spare vehicles. Have him give me a call. I'll hammer out a good price so you'll be free of those payments as well."

The pit of her stomach ached so badly she was afraid she would throw up. It was all too much to take. Too much to handle. Damn him and his father for allowing her to get into this situation.

Michael waited beside her chair. She didn't look like she was going to leave. He scrubbed his hand through his hair and sat on the edge of his desk. "I'm sorry you're in this predicament. It's not a lost cause. Yet. But it is going to require major changes to your lifestyle."

She tipped her gorgeous face up and looked at him. Her sparkling-blue eyes swam with unshed tears, making his heart squeeze harder. While he knew he wasn't to blame for her situation, he couldn't help feeling sorry for her. "I know. It's not easy. You're made of pretty tough stuffing. You can survive this. But it's going to take a lot of fiscal restraint."

She looked down at the one hundred dollar bill and the two cards in her trembling hand. Her head bobbed slightly. "I've always been able to get whatever I want, whenever I want it."

His arms fell to his sides, palms forward, fingers spread. "I know. Perhaps you can bounce back and return to your old ways, eventually." He sincerely hoped that wouldn't be the case. But chances were that she would return to her normal behavior. She'd been born into a life of financial abundance. Money was an object to be spent. Not something to save, not even for a rainy day. Because it didn't rain in her world. Not until now.

In slow motion, she picked up her purse, opened it, and stuffed the money and cards inside. It snapped shut with a metallic click. When she stood, Michael led her to the office door.

She moved more slowly, like a sleepwalker in a trance. It was eerie after how she had stomped in, demanding to know what was going on. Opening the door, he stopped her. "I will be calling daily to see how you're doing." Then he remembered her plan to find someone to marry. "Let me know how your quest to find love goes."

Her eyes met his again, this time filled with fury. "I'm not looking for love. All I need is a husband."

Michael watched her leave. She was something else in so many different ways. There were times he wanted to hold her, hug her, assure her she could do this. Other times, she was a spoiled brat who needed to have the haughty entitlement shaken out of her. She was so used to getting everything she wanted. This time would be different.

Moving to the window, he watched her get into her Mustang and drive away. He sighed, glad to have finally addressed the situation with her. There had been many sleepless nights worrying about this confrontation.

He stared at the portrait of his father on the wall. The dull ache in his chest increased. Most times, he missed him and wished he had survived. Other times, he cursed his father for letting the business get into this mess. His father and the business had put him in a precarious spot. He hadn't wanted to change his life either. His father's rapidly deteriorating health had forced him to quit a job he enjoyed and move back home. Forced him to give up his independence and the condo he loved in Stowe. Everything had been packed up and placed in storage for a day he wasn't sure would ever return. It was the only way he could keep the business and his family financially stable. If only for a little while.

Returning to his desk, he noticed she hadn't taken the balance sheet vividly showing her ruined finances. Plucking it from the desktop, he stuffed it into her file and stowed it away in his top center desk drawer.

Flopping down in his chair, he closed his eyes and hung his head. The image of her when she was ten or eleven materialized in his mind. She'd taken away his pre-teen breath with one look. Her blonde hair was so fair it was almost white. Her pre-pubescent body was narrow, petite, and ethereal, like a hummingbird's. Her perfect nose, porcelain skin, and barely pink lips were perfection. It was her eyes that struck him in the chest like an arrow. Grecian blue, as he liked to consider them, clear and worldly. Even back then, her manner was ostentatious.

He smiled and snorted. It was probably a good thing he hadn't yet hit full puberty back then otherwise that look might have given him his first hard-on.

After that episode, he always tried to sneak a peek at his father's appointment calendar. If he saw Senator Perret was scheduled, he'd try to be in his father's office. Just for another look at his daughter. She never came back.

The vision of her on that first meeting never left him. It was the stuff of his deepest secrets and dreams. While nothing had ever happened between them, he never forgot her. And he never got an opportunity to pursue her. *Well, except for that one incident in college.*

CHAPTER FOUR

She couldn't remember driving back home, parking the Mustang, or entering the house. *Did I disable the alarm system?* She must have because she was standing in her living room and the alarm wasn't sounding.

Flopping her purse on the sofa table, she slipped off her Casadei stilettos, her bare feet sinking into the deep plush pile of the beige carpet. She went to her small desk beside the window and sat. *Staring out the window isn't going to get this done any faster.*

Caroline turned on her cell phone and opened her texts. There were messages, all of them from her gala tablemates. The words blurred as she read them:

Where are you?

Did you check into a different hotel? The front desk says you never arrived and our rooms were canceled.

You didn't show up for drinks at the bar last night. What's going on?

Wiping her tears, she started composing a group message.

> "Dear friends, I became ill on the way to the city. Had the chauffeur take me back home. I don't know if it's something contagious, so I'm staying home. Have a great time at the gala. "

Well, at least some of my message was true. She stared at it, her finger unwilling to hit the send icon. *No time like the present.* Placing her finger on the key, she closed her eyes and pressed.

She made sure it had gone out to all the right people. There was nothing she could do. There was no other recourse. The finality of the message felt like a door closing on an event she had been nurturing for the last year. She might never get another opportunity to buy another table. Not with the status of her finances right now.

Stop procrastinating and finish the job.

Caroline tapped at her phone and entered the long list of her travel friends in the To line. Staring at the blank space awaiting her, she tried to compose the next message. She chewed at her lower lip for a few minutes before deciding on the wording.

"Due to circumstances beyond my control, I've had to cancel our forthcoming trips to Europe."

She stared at the blinking cursor, frowned, and deleted the entire sentence.

As far as her girlfriends knew, their first of three trips to Europe was still leaving in seven weeks for the Tour de France. Not that they liked biking or followed it. All of them were hoping to find themselves husbands during the male-only event, or at the very least, some sexual escapades. Canceling the trip was going to disappoint everyone. Including me, she thought with a heavy heart.

Staring at the text box, Caroline thought harder. If she canceled all three trips at once, everyone would ask why. There had to be a way to cancel that wouldn't draw suspicion. The last thing she wanted to do was tell them she was on the verge of bankruptcy. Perhaps she could cancel the first France trip? Maybe she would have that trust fund money by the time the other two trips came about. And she wouldn't lose her friends.

Caroline had always considered her friends steady throughout college. Their fair-weather loyalty became evident when everything had gone down with her wedding and the incident at the Canadian border. Many had been scarce afterward. They didn't reply to her texts or voice messages. It wasn't until a few months ago that they had started coming around again. Right when Caroline was organizing her European trips. She had invited the few who had remained friendly. Suddenly, word must have spread. Soon, she was inundated with messages from those who had distanced themselves from her. Each of them hinting at an invitation.

She sighed again, dismissing their fickle nature from her mind. Her decision made, she tapped out the message with her thumbs, adding a heart emoji at the end.

> "With regret, I've discovered a scheduling conflict for our next trip to France. I'm sorry to say I have had to cancel the trip. My sincere apologies."

She double-checked that everyone scheduled for the trip was listed as a recipient before she hit send and collapsed against the back of her chair. It was done.

Over the next couple of hours, her friends lamented the trip's cancelation or the illness preventing her from going to the Met. None seemed to suspect the real reason. Some on the trip had been a little snippy about the cancelation. *Screw them.* Caroline knew many were not real friends. Not like Rachel. Only Rachel Evangeline, her BFF from Smith College, had questioned the cancelation.

Caroline put off the question, answering,

> I'll tell you later.

Hours later, she sat on her bed binging on ice cream instead of sweeping down the red carpet and up the marble stairs of the Metropolitan Museum of Art. Her spoon dipped into the pint of Ben & Jerry's Phish Food as tears spilled down her face, the glow of the enormous TV screen on the wall illuminating her lotus posture on the bed. The center of her chest ached. This could have been her best night ever. Instead, she sat in her silk pajamas, watching the gala red carpet live feed of celebrities posing and primping for the cameras.

QUEST FOR LOVE

After a short time, she became so engrossed with the images that her tears stopped. She oohed and ahhed over the celebrities and the costumes they wore. Some were totally drab, way too tame for the event's theme, which was opulence and excess. Pretending she was a judge on *Project Runway*, she pulled a note pad out from her bedside table and gave each carpet walker a numerical score for their costume.

The fun kept her mind off her misery until the Sardash twins arrived. Her spoon dropped into the almost empty ice cream carton as she watched the two people she had wanted to meet. Meeting them was the entire reason for attending the gala. Her eyes welled with tears again as her breath caught in her chest. Swiping her eyes to clear her vision, she couldn't help but notice how amazing they looked in their elaborate plumed outfits, one resembling a peacock and the other a toucan.

When the camera panned over to the next arrival, she shut off the TV, flopped down on the bed face first, and blubbered like a baby.

CHAPTER FIVE

Her accountant called mid-morning the next day, interrupting her hour-long yoga practice. "How's it going?"

"Not good. My face is disfigured from crying last night." Caroline wanted him to feel bad for forcing her into this budgeting plan. "It broke my heart to watch all the gala excitement on TV when I had a table and a ticket to be there in person."

"I'm sorry that didn't work out. But if you had answered our emails, texts, voice messages, and letters, we wouldn't be quite where we are today."

Fire shot through her entire body. How dare he accuse her of being neglectful. "Shouldn't you have contacted me earlier?" she barked. "Do you take pleasure in destroying my life?"

Mr. DuBois snorted. "Don't blame me, I'm just the messenger. Would you rather spend the last of your money, go bankrupt, or worse—get arrested for stealing."

Caroline thought her head was going to blow off. "Stealing! Why stealing? I've never stolen anything in my life!" Her teeth ground together as she simmered in indignation.

His voice remained the same calm, matter-of-fact tone as before. "If you buy something you can't afford to pay for, even as credit card payments, then it's technically stealing. How would that look for your father if you were arrested like your former fiancé?"

"Screw my father and his precious reputation." She paced the length of the living room, feeling her heart pounding. It would take her hours to get calm enough to resume her peaceful yoga session. As it was, her body felt overheated in her yoga clothes. "I didn't know what was happening."

"Of course, you didn't. You buried your head in the sand. That doesn't absolve you of the situation." He changed his tactic suddenly. "How much of that one hundred dollars do you have left?"

"All of it. I had such a headache after our meeting yesterday I had to come straight home. I spent the afternoon emailing my friends about the gala and trip cancellations. I had to take a sleeping pill to get any rest last night."

"Don't you mean trips, as in multiple?"

Caroline cringed. Mr. DuBois had caught her. "I only canceled the first trip. I should be married and rolling in money again before the other trips come up. One is in August, and the other is in September. Those should be able to go on as planned."

"Hmm, I see. Have you found anyone yet?" The tone of Mr. DuBois's voice told her he had no faith in her plan.

"I was going to work on that project after my yoga workout." A sneer crept into her voice, "So if you don't mind, I'd like to get back to work."

"Speaking of work—" he started to say.

She cringed. *Why did you use that word?* "Tomorrow," Caroline hissed.

"Fine, fine. I'll call for an update tomorrow," Mr. DuBois said before abruptly hanging up.

Caroline started her yoga sequences all over from the beginning but found her balance was significantly compromised by her smoldering thoughts. Giving up, she laid back on her yoga mat in shavasana. She hated being interrupted and harassed. She would tackle the online dating website after she showered and changed.

CHAPTER SIX

The Biography box on the cell phone screen was blank. Caroline had been staring at the lazily flashing cursor like it would suddenly erupt in a flurry of words for more than twenty minutes. A phrase assembled itself in her brain. Her thumbs rose, poised over the keyboard. She huffed and put her phone back down in her lap. Nope.

The ringtone "Independent Women" sounded, signaling it was Rachel Evangeline. Caroline debated whether she should answer. It would break her concentration just when she was trying to focus. Too late.

"Hello, Rach," Caroline said, putting the call on speaker while still staring at Single and Free, a dating app for adults under the age of thirty.

"Caroline, where have you been? We were supposed to meet at The Dockside for lunch thirty minutes ago," Rachel said in an exasperated voice. "First you back out of the Met Gala. Then you cancel the France trip. And now you stand me up? What's up girl?"

Caroline cringed involuntarily and slumped in her chair. She didn't want to have to explain her situation. Better not to speak of it and concentrate on finding someone to marry ... and quickly. Before she was forced to tell Rachel she was broke. Because telling Rachel would be the same as telling every one of their friends. Much as she loved her, she recognized Rachel couldn't keep a secret. Except for one massive secret, for which Caroline was grateful.

Should she admit she forgot the time? But what reason? Telling her she didn't show because she couldn't pick up the check like always was unthinkable. It would flag Rachel's suspicion. "I'm sorry. I'm not feeling myself. I've been forgetting everything. I missed my hair appointment, my massage, and my mani/pedi. It's not just you." Her fingers played with the hem of her soft cotton jersey dress.

QUEST FOR LOVE

"Huh. Why? I mean, I know you can be forgetful, but you've never missed one of our lunches."

Caroline cringed again. "I, um, I'm in the middle of filling out a form online, and I got sucked down the rabbit hole."

"What form could possibly be more important than your weekly lunch with me?" Rachel chuckled. Then she waited for Caroline's reply.

The silence wedged between them as Caroline contemplated the pros and cons of telling Rachel she'd downloaded a dating app.

"Well?" Rachel's tone held an edge this time. An edge Caroline didn't want to traverse.

"I'm signing up on a dating app."

All Caroline heard was her friend gasp. This time, Rachel let the silence hang between them like a vacuum.

"I'm tired of being alone. I'm looking for a husband, if you must know." She crossed her fingers, hoping the declaration would change the dynamic of the conversation.

"What!" Rachel screeched. "Are you serious?"

Caroline sighed. "Yes. I'm looking for my soul mate." She had no real understanding of what that meant, but she thought it sounded good.

"I'm speechless," Rachel said.

"That's a first. Let me write this down in my journal." Caroline bit back the colorful language she wanted to use. No sense in alienating Rachel. She might be the only friend still talking to her since she had to cancel the trip.

"Why now? You fled your wedding before the I do's less than a year ago." Her voice darkened with suspicion.

"David doesn't count. I didn't love him. I was always suspicious of his motives. As it turned out, my gut was right." David Hayes Wescott and Caroline Rose Perret had nearly been married seven months ago. Just days after she backed out, he and half his family had been arrested for fraud. "It was a lucky intuition."

Just talking about the near miss sent shivers up her spine. She had suspected all along that David only wanted access to her trust fund. His and his family's arrest had born out the truth.

"I'll say. It was the only time I've seen your mother cry." Rachel paused a second before adding, "Tell me about the website."

Caroline rolled her eyes as her shoulders slumped. She had hoped the David fiasco would distract Rachel, but she was like a dog with a bone. No, scratch that. A cat playing with a mouse was a better description. "It's basic. I signed up and paid for the first month."

"Hmm, maybe I should give it a try. Lord knows the guys we hang with aren't interested in marriage."

Thank God. "Why would they be when they have oodles of money to purchase their every whim."

"I don't get it. Weren't you trying to stay away from sex and physical intimacy?"

It was true. Caroline didn't want a sexual partner. She wanted a platonic husband. She *would* find one. Caroline stared at her phone screen. "I'm trying to write a short bio for my profile page."

"That's easy. Let's see … I'd say 'Beautiful, carefree, rich, generous fashion icon and Vermont socialite. Likes to party, take her friends on long exotic vacations around the world and buy them all presents. Health and fitness conscious for her slim figure.' How does that sound?"

"I don't want to mention being rich. I want to find a man who will love me as a normal woman."

"But you're not normal." Rachel giggled this time. "What picture did you use?"

She jumped up from her chair and dug her fingers into her hair. "Look, I've got to go."

"Fine, but let me know who you hook up with." Rachel called out before hanging up, "Oh! Are you going to meet me for lunch next week?"

QUEST FOR LOVE

She stopped her pacing. "I'll let you know."

Caroline disconnected, thankful Rachel hadn't asked about the reason behind the trip cancelation. She contemplated the blank white space still waiting for her self-description. What Rachel had said about her made her feel content. She had cultivated that persona for so long that she believed it herself. It was too late to change.

She placed her thumbs on the keys and wrote what came to mind.

"Conscientious and carefree!

This fashion icon and Vermont socialite likes to party, travel with friends, and attend social events. Health and fitness conscious, environmentally friendly, and an admirer of the finer things in life. Looking for a SWM husband."

After re-reading the blurb several times, she hit upload. She had already uploaded a picture from her last trip to the Greek islands. It was a profile headshot, but she was clearly wearing a bathing suit. Her tanned face and bare shoulders dazzled, her sunglasses hid her eyes, and her sun hat shaded her features. All except for the straight blonde hair which framed her face.

Within five minutes, she had several notifications from Victor K, Daring Daryl, and Kyle, The Lifeguard. All three looked to be in their late twenties; all were handsome enough, neat, and clean-shaven.

The rest of her afternoon was spent messaging back and forth with the three men. Before she closed the app to go to dinner with her older brother, she had three dates scheduled over the next two weeks, starting tomorrow night with Victor. It seemed rather ambitious but she didn't have a lot of time. If the first date worked out, she could cancel the other two.

CHAPTER SEVEN

Regina's condo buzzed with activity. Sitting at the dining table, Caroline noted it looked far more cluttered since Tony moved in six months ago. The cathedral ceiling gave the living room and adjacent dining area a spacious feel. The French doors were blocked with shelving holding indoor houseplants in various containers. Three cats lounged on the couch, unperturbed by the bustling.

Tony's desk was against the far wall, stacked with papers and books. His work as a senior public policy advisor with Vermont's civil rights office, he was permitted to work from home. The last Caroline heard, he was working to free up public access to some of Vermont's best trout streams in the Northeast Kingdom.

To Caroline's surprise, Tony flitted about the kitchen, still in his office attire but with his shirt sleeves rolled up. He was trying to get the table set while Regina put the meal together.

A black cat stretched and jumped off the couch. It came over, looking up at her from beside her chair. Seeing the cat checking her out, she leaned down and let it sniff her hand. The cat head-butted her knuckles, so she petted him hesitantly while the other two cautiously watched from the safety of the couch.

"I thought you didn't like animals," Regina said, her red and white gingham apron strings fluttering as she sped by, heading for the pantry closet.

Caroline marveled at Regina's flower print dress. It had a small and playful bow at the bottom of the zipper near her lower back. "I don't really. This one is calm enough and seems friendly. As long as they don't bite or scratch me or try to jump up onto my clothes, I'll be okay." As if Rascal was waiting for a cue, the cat jumped onto Caroline's lap as soon as she sat back in her chair. Caroline cringed, her body tense, her hands fisted, and her arms covering the center of her chest. "Get it down," she begged Tony. Tony batted at the cat, forcing it to leave Caroline's lap. "Thank you," Caroline said, her hands already trying to dust off the black cat hairs from her white jeans and pink cashmere sweater. *This cat hair problem is the real reason I dislike cats, well, any animal, really.*

She sipped at the wine Tony had poured for her. A perfectly blended rosé from the Rhone region of France. Lightly chilled and high on the alcohol content, it soothed her mind. She sighed, watching her brother and his wife come together and break apart to opposite ends of the kitchen. Swirling around each other, they never actually met face to face. Instead, they passed by or reached out but didn't touch. It reminded Caroline of a dance company she had seen in New York City the week before her world collided with the brick wall of pending insolvency. Cringing at the memory, she sought a distraction. "How was your honeymoon?" Caroline asked, taking another sip of her wine.

"It was great. We did a lot of sightseeing and fly-fished in a different river every day." Tony's hand passed a plate beneath her nose.

Regina added, "You should go. It's beautiful."

"I don't think Scotland's quite my style. I'd rather be in Paris, or Milan, or Vienna." Her mind flickered to Paris. It would be beautiful this time of year with all the flowers blooming. She itched suddenly to make hotel and flight reservations. *Not this year,* she sighed.

"Earth to Caroline," Tony muttered as he set the plate on the placemat before her. Flatware clinked as he deposited her utensils beside the paper napkin.

"Hmm. Sorry. I was thinking back to a performance I saw weeks before this fiasco started." Her fingers played with the stem of the delicate crystal wine goblet before she took another sip.

"What happened a month before?" Tony watched her intently before reaching for his wineglass and sipping.

"I attended a modern dance performance in New York City. Watching you two navigate around each other in the kitchen reminded me of one of the dances."

Tony raised an eyebrow as he set his glass down. "I see."

Caroline knew he didn't see. It was one of her last business-as-usual trips. Only weeks later, her life had changed. Temporarily, she hoped. "Don't mind me. I'm still in shock. I can't believe three million dollars could disappear so fast."

Her brother shook his head. "I suggested you invest all of it for a reason. You could have lived comfortably off the interest for a while." He frowned. "Now, you have nothing to live on."

Regina, minus the apron, brought the platter of pork roast, lying on a thick bed of roasted beets, carrots, and butternut squash. "Dinner is served."

Tony and Regina took their places at the table. Regina spooned a little of everything as they held their plates out. "What's this I hear about your accountant?"

"Oh, Henry DuBois had some sort of sudden illness and passed away. His son, Michael, has assumed the business." Caroline cut a small wedge of fat off the edge of her pork slice.

"He's a CPA, then?" Regina asked.

Caroline looked up in surprise. "I didn't even ask." She chewed on a small bite of meat. "I think he is. Seems to me Henry mentioned several times he hoped his son would follow in his footsteps."

"What are you going to do about the situation?"

"Mr. DuBois advised me to sell all but one of my cars, cancel my vacation trips, and put the townhouse up for sale before the bank forecloses."

As Caroline watched, Regina and Tony passed a look between them. Both looked aghast. Tony spoke up, "Where are you going to live?"

"I don't know. I'm certainly not going to ask to move back in with Mom and Dad." She shuddered at the thought.

Tony scowled. "I can't fault you there. I'd rather live on the streets than go crawling back to them." He gave her an apologetic nod. "There isn't enough room here. Besides, this isn't my condo."

"Is your condo still let?" Regina asked Tony, her voice filled with genuine curiosity.

Tony's face brightened. "The current tenants notified me they would be relocating for new jobs soon. They said they would be moving to Maine."

"Have you found a new tenant yet?" Caroline gave him a silent, pleading look.

He shrugged. "I don't know. I'm not even sure of the timing. I'll give the property management company a call." He reached out and squeezed her hand. "If not, I can let it to you on a month-by-month basis."

Caroline's heart surged with love that her brother would do that for her. "I'd be grateful for it. But I don't know when I can pay you." Shuffling her veggies from one side of the plate to the other, piece by piece, Caroline added, "That's the other advice. Mr. Dubois wants me to get a job."

Tony glanced up, making Caroline groan at his look of surprise. "That's not a bad idea, no matter your financial situation." A smirk spread across his face. "Have you ever had a job? Like ever?"

Regina pressed her lips together to stifle her own smirk as Caroline glared at the two of them.

"Not exactly. I did help the cook at Mom and Dad's house here in Fulton River."

"Yeah, when you were like—five, maybe." Tony's chuckle rang out, filling the dining space.

The heat of indignation crept through Caroline's bones again. Why did everyone always make fun of her for never having had a job? She knew she was capable of work. Just because she didn't prefer to spend her time doing what someone else wanted her to do didn't mean she didn't know how. "I could get a job. But I'm not going to need one."

The light clatter of flatware on the dishes stopped as Tony and Regina looked at each other again in silent communication. Really, that's rather rude, Caroline thought.

"How are you going to solve the problem?" Regina asked finally, taking a sip of wine.

"I'm going to get married. In a hurry." Caroline smiled smugly. "Grandma's trust will solve all my problems when I get married. With a prenup, of course."

Again, her brother and his wife shared a not-so-secret look across the table. Tony cleared his throat before asking the obvious question. "Who will you marry? Do you have someone in mind?"

"No, but I'm sure lots of men would jump at the chance to marry me," she replied with a shake of her head.

That look again passed between her brother and his wife. Regina continued the inquisition, "Where are you going to find this man?"

"I signed up on a dating app last night and already have sixteen followers and three dates lined up."

Caroline's utensils clattered into her plate as their silent communication started again. She huffed, "Would you two stop that!"

Tony set down his utensils. "Caro, that's not a great idea. There are plenty of creeps out there, usually looking for an encounter. Not a date."

"I'm twenty-two years old. I think I can manage my own affairs." She sent both of them a fiery look she hoped they recognized as a reproach.

Regina and Tony's eyebrows rose in unison, incredulous looks on their faces.

He picked up his fork. "Hmm. If that were true, how come you're in this predicament?"

She cringed inside. He had a point there. Her decision-making history wasn't the best. First, there was Randy. Then there was David. Both had been very bad decisions. And now there was the financial debacle.

"I let people run my affairs. I let Mom push me into marrying David. I won't let that happen again."

"I still think you should get that job as Mr. DuBois's son suggested. You could use a dose of reality."

"You know," Regina started, "If you want something light and easy, you could come work with me. You can start out part-time in the Fulton store. It would give you an idea of what it's like to have one. A job, that is."

Caroline shoved her plate aside before gently patting her lips with her napkin. She liked her sister-in-law. It was Caroline's insistence that Gina Blooms provide the flowers for her almost wedding that reunited Tony and Regina. "That's very thoughtful of you, but I don't think that's quite my speed."

Regina nodded slowly. "I didn't mean to insult you. It's just that someone who has never had a job before might find it hard to get used to doing one."

"I get your point. I just think the work is beneath me." She gazed up at the ceiling in thought. "I think maybe being a fashion designer or interior decorator would be more my style."

Tony started choking on the sip of water he'd just taken. Regina leaned over and slapped his back none too gently. When he caught his breath again, he asked in a raspy voice, "What qualifications do you possess to get such a job?"

Caroline looked at him coolly. "Experience. I have a wonderful fashion sense. Everyone says so. My townhouse was in the *Vermont Home Décor* magazine. Everyone loveé how I decorated it."

Regina gave her a nod. "True. Well, good luck in your job hunt. If you change your mind, you know where to find me. My offer stands."

CHAPTER EIGHT

As she promised Mr. DuBois, she started making phone calls the following day.

"Hello. Can I speak with the manager?" Caroline asked the person who answered at the Montpelier store, INTERIORS. She was put on hold for the office manager.

"Yes, how can I help you?" the woman answered when she got on the phone.

Caroline ignored the flutter of butterflies in her gut and proceeded with the speech she had memorized. "Hello, I'm Caroline Perret. I'm looking for a job in the interior decorator field. Do you have anything open?" Her teeth were gnawing at her lower lip so hard it might bleed. But she couldn't stop it.

"I could always use a new decorator. Where did you get your training?"

"I'm self-taught," Caroline replied with more confidence than she felt at the moment.

There was a brief pause before the woman said, "Hmm. I see. Do you have experience with art and design or color theory? Or historical designs?"

"Uh ... well. Um, I decorated my entire townhouse," Caroline said.

"Really." The lilt in the woman's voice sounded like sarcasm. "So you never attended a program accredited by Certified Interior Decorators International or Interior Design Society?"

She closed her eyes in exasperation. "No, but my work was showcased in *Vermont Home Décor* magazine."

"Hmm, really? That's extraordinary." There was definitely a bite to the woman's words. "Do you have a portfolio of your work?"

"The magazine has lots of pictures that prove my talent." She didn't want to let the woman know she didn't have a portfolio. She had never decorated anyone else's house.

"I'm sorry. We need *experienced* interior decorators. Not someone who learned at Pottery Loft or Crate and Craft. Give me another call when you have the proper training and a portfolio. Bub-bye." The line clicked and went dead.

Fire raged in her gut, threatening to explode out her ears. "I'll never call you again," she said into the phone before disconnecting.

Looking at her list of six interior decorator shops, she dialed the next one. That call ended exactly as the first, except the owner cackled hysterically before hanging up.

Caroline tried the next, and the next, and the next. After getting essentially the same response each time, she crumpled up the paper and threw it toward the waste basket. It hit the rim then bounced out onto the carpet. Her eyes rolled.

"I guess I'll try fashion design. That should be a lot easier." She started on the list of fashion boutiques in Montpelier and Brattleboro. The job inquiries went nearly identical to the last five, only worse. Each place wanted a bachelor's degree in a program that studied fabrics, fashion history, fashion theory as well as color theory. They also asked if she knew computer-aided fashion design software, which, of course, she didn't. She'd never heard of it.

Cradling her head in her hands, she tried to stifle the tears threatening to seep under her lids. *What a way to start the day.* How was she going to explain to Mr. DuBois that she had no work skills? If he didn't ask her directly, she wouldn't mention the job hunt.

Mr. DuBois called just after her yogurt with flaxseed lunch. Caroline answered on the fifth ring. Really, the man called her every day. *Does he have to keep such a close watch on me?*

"Ms. Perret. How is it going?"

"It's going just fine. I have a date tonight with a guy. He looks promising."

The line was silent for a number of seconds. "No. I was talking about selling your extra vehicles. Putting your townhouse up for sale. Did you contact the car salesman and the real estate agent?"

Caroline's eyes rolled as she shook her head. "No need, Mr. DuBois. I have everything under control. You'll be hearing Mendelssohn's wedding march in a few weeks."

"Ms. Perret. I had to make the next mortgage payment on your townhouse. You really can't afford to make another. You have less than four weeks to get everything settled."

The exasperation in his voice stirred Caroline's ire. A hot flame shot straight up her spine. "Mr. DuBois, that's plenty of time. All I'll need is a couple of dates, a trip to town hall, and a justice of the peace. I can be married in minutes. Do not fret."

"Don't fret?" His voice dripped with incredulity. "Are you kidding me? No! No! You're kidding yourself. You don't have a clue. Do you really want to hitch yourself to any warm-bodied, breathing male just to secure the last of your trust fund?"

"Of course not. I'm being very selective about this. Each man has to have a job. Be in the correct age range—not younger than me, up to about thirty-five. That's my limit. God knows I don't want to be responsible for caretaking someone elderly."

"Thirty-five? Elderly?" Again, his voice rose an octave higher. "Ms. Perret, I implore you to be reasonable. At least get that luxury townhouse of yours listed with an agent." Shouting, he added, "And get a job."

Caroline could not believe her ears. "Stop telling me what to do."

"Look, you hired this firm to oversee your finances. My father worked tirelessly this past year trying to help you understand you needed to be smarter about your spending—"

"Don't chastise me. You work for me. Don't forget that."

"Oh, no." His voice sounded vicious. "I don't work for you. You haven't had enough money to pay your accounting fees for the last three months. You currently owe this firm well over eight thousand dollars for back payments and all the additional work and trouble you've perpetrated." He cleared his throat before going on, "Not to mention all the pain and suffering trying to straighten this mess out. That's money this company needs to pay its employees."

Caroline sat back in her chair, stunned. There was no other word for it. All this time, she thought she had been paying for the accounting services. "I—" She swallowed hard and started again, still not knowing what to say to this man. This pigheaded bully of an accountant. She pictured his face at their last meeting. He was terribly handsome, very fit. He clearly looked after himself. "I'm sorry. I didn't know," she whispered into the phone so quietly he might not have even heard her words.

"Well..." The tone of his voice was back to normal. "I'm sorry. I'm sure this has come as a terrible shock to you. I'm trying desperately to keep you out of foreclosure and bankruptcy. Trying to keep your name and situation out of the newspapers. You and I both know what would happen if the reporters knew what was happening to Senator Perret's daughter." She would never hear the end of her father's rantings if it became known his daughter was bankrupt. His constituents as well as the rest of the United States Senate, would never let him forget it.

Her jaw went tight, realizing she was having to tailor her actions to uphold his senatorial and social status. A huge sinking feeling overwhelmed her at failing yet again to live her life as she pleased without consideration for her parents. After all they did to her. Caroline heaved a long, heavy sigh. "Please. Please forgive me. I'll—" She stopped, not wanting to say the words. Because saying them might make it so. "I'll contact the car salesman. I rarely drive the Jag, Astin Martin, or the Hummer. They should garner a tidy sum. Perhaps enough to pay what I owe you at the very least."

"Not likely. Let's concentrate on freeing you from those car payments." He sighed. "I know this is difficult, Ms. Perret. But please remember, I'm trying to help you."

Another awkward silence.

It seemed odd to her that here was this man, a young man, filling in for his father. His father had been very good to her over the last year. Ever since she received that trust fund money. She had grown very fond of him. He'd asked her to call him Henry on their first meeting. Now, it occurred to her that she had never asked his son to call her by her given name. The dull ache of regret blossomed in her gut.

"Mr. DuBois?"

"Yes, Ms. Perret? I'm still here."

"Your name is Michael. Michael DeBois, isn't it?"

"Yes, why?"

For some reason, saying his name clicked in the back of her brain. She remembered meeting a Michael DuBois at a party. "I'd like to call you Michael. Would you call me Caroline?"

He hesitated before replying, "Yes."

"Did we ever meet in college? Maybe a few years ago?" she asked tentatively, unsure how much information to divulge in case it hadn't been him.

"I believe we did. At an Epsilon Nu Tau event at UMass. I believe you were in Smith at the time."

"True. That was quite a party. Crashing UMass parties was the only means my friends and I could meet guys."

"Right. I forgot Smith is a women's college."

Silence again as both of them digested the shared encounter two years before.

"How's the one hundred holding out?"

"I haven't used any of it yet. But I'll need to go shopping tomorrow for some groceries."

"Okay. Be very judicious. There are four more days left in the week."

"I'm aware of that," she sighed purposefully. For now, she was going to have to concede. "I'll see about a job, Michael."

"Thank you, Caroline."

The connection broke, leaving Caroline staring off into space, her mind trying to peel back the years. Rachel and a half dozen of their friends had crashed the party looking for guys. They coerced her to go with them. What could she say that wouldn't sound suspicious? Rachel knew why she didn't want to go, but the others didn't. Nor was she willing to tell them. It was easier to go and flirt but not allow any male to get too close. Or think he was getting attached. If she remembered correctly, Michael had tried to flirt with her. She smiled and flirted lightly, then moved on. It was easier to be a social butterfly than give a guy the wrong impression. The impression she was looking for a pickup.

Then it occurred to her that Mr. DuBois, Michael, had called her by her first name.

CHAPTER NINE

The arrangement was to meet Victor outside the new Mexican restaurant on School Street, not far from the Fulton River Falls. She ditched her usual Jaguar for the Range Rover. It still spoke loudly of money but was less showy than the Jag, Hummer, or Astin Martin. The Hummer mostly sat in the garage. It was too big to park along the narrow Fulton River city streets and parking lots. How people ever parked big bruising cars like caddies or station wagons in the 60s and 70s, she had no idea.

Victor had described himself as twenty-nine, six foot two inches tall, thin, bespectacled, with dark brown hair and dark brown eyes. His photo showed a smiling man of the appropriate age wearing a baseball cap and some kind of team jersey.

As she approached the exterior door, it opened from the inside by a man who loosely resembled the description she had been given. Except this guy wasn't six foot two, but he might actually be sixty-two. He wasn't thin either. His flannel-clad beer belly extended over the belt on his well-worn jeans. While he was wearing glasses, what might have been dark brown hair glimmered with extensive gray-white highlights. Not just a few at the temples. But diffusely through his entire head of hair.

The loud voice in her brain told her to return to her car and get the hell out of there. It would be rude to ghost him, but if this really were him, he'd falsely portrayed himself. A tiny voice reminded her that this might not be Victor.

The man held the door open, waiting for her to approach. He smiled broadly, a glint in his dark brown eyes. At least his eye color was true. "Caroline?"

Putting on her best fake smile, she nodded. "Yes. I'm Caroline. Are you Victor?"

QUEST FOR LOVE

He beamed. "Yes, I am. I knew this was going to be my lucky day. My horoscope told me so."

Caroline smiled back, a twitch already forming in her right eye. "My, my. I had no idea."

"Come on then. I've got the waitress holding us a quiet table for two in the corner. Cost me five bucks to get her to save it for us."

Five? The wait staff or hostess required twenty or more to save the best table anywhere she had ever gone.

When the hostess led them to a table in the center of the gigantic dining area, Caroline nearly busted out laughing. Victor tried arguing with the woman, reminding her under his breath about the tip he'd given her to save the table. He even pointed at the table, frowning as he saw a younger couple checking out menus as they sat at what he considered his table.

"I'm so sorry about that. A waitress must have given them that table when I was in the kitchen straightening out a problem." The tiny smirk gave her away. But Victor wasn't watching. His eyes were riveted to the table he lost.

"I gave you a tip," He muttered again under his breath, trying not to move his lips.

The hostess shrugged. "I'm so sorry," she said before looking over at the door. "Excuse me, I have to greet the customers."

Caroline sat down while Victor still stood beside the table, his eyes narrowing as he watched the other people at *his* table place their orders with a waitress. The way he stared at them worried her. Would he take matters into his own hands and demand the table? As it was, he was making a spectacle of himself, refusing to sit down.

Whispering and glances started at the surrounding tables, like rubberneckers at an accident site. Caroline ignored his weird behavior, concentrating on the decor of the restaurant. The barn-like structure with exposed beams, the authentic-looking wicker baskets, and the stereotypical Mexican items like piñatas, multicolored pottery, and rough-woven blankets. Unable to stand it any longer, she said, "Victor, have a seat. This table is nice."

He scowled at her before roughly pulling out his chair and sitting. "I don't know what makes me madder: seeing that other couple at *our* table or the hostess not giving me my five dollars back."

Caroline blinked a few times, unable to believe this guy could get hung up on such a silly issue. And her humor got the better of her when she couldn't stop herself from saying, "But it's your lucky day, so perhaps fate has something better in store for you at this table." She smiled as prettily as she could.

He shrugged, flicked his napkin out, and laid it on his lap. "That must be it. The cards don't lie."

"So true," Caroline assured him before picking up her menu. *I think I should order the most expensive entrée on the menu, just to spite this ass.*

The same waitress arrived and described a few specials before asking for their drink order.

"No, thank you," Victor interjected before she could say anything.

Caroline ignored him. "I'd love a Herodes Mezcal if you have it."

The waitress nodded. "With sour orange and worm salt?"

Caroline smiled. "Of course."

After the waitress walked away, Caroline stole a glance at Victor in her peripheral vision. He was scowling again. His face had reddened.

"What the heck is worm salt?" he blurted.

"Just what it sounds like. It's sea salt, toasted, ground up agave worms, and dried chilies."

His nose wrinkled. "Disgusting."

The small ceramic bowl of mezcal arrived with a plate of orange slices and a small square tile. The waitress pulled out an herb bottle and sprinkled the tile with the worm salt. She smiled at Caroline, shot Victor a hard glance, and said, "Enjoy!"

Caroline picked up the tiny ceramic bowl and took an equally tiny sip. Her eyes widened. It was delicious. She wiggled her eyebrows at him before picking up an orange slice, dipping it into the worm salt, and eating the orange flesh.

A horrified look erupted on his face as he sat back. "I can't believe you ate that wormy stuff."

Caroline grinned. "What? It's good." She held out an orange slice and gently pushed the tile toward him.

His hands flew up palms forward. "No way."

"Suit yourself." She picked up her menu again. "Shall we order appetizers?"

Forcefully, Victor said, "No. Let's just order an entrée."

She looked at him, silent. Was he really suggesting they only order one entrée for the both of them? Her eyes scanned the menu for an entrée for two. It wasn't inconceivable that this place had something like that. There wasn't any on the menu.

Victor must have taken her silence for approval. "I suggest the shrimp fajitas." At the expression on her face, he quickly added, "You don't have a shrimp allergy, do you?"

"Umm, no. I'd like to get a taco salad. But by all means, get the shrimp for yourself."

His eyes narrowed before he took her hand. "I thought it would be more romantic if we shared one plate."

The mezcal was super strong. It was an agave liquor along the same lines as tequila. She had, by now, finished her drink and half the oranges. Her lips were feeling a little loose, which was probably why she muttered, "Romantic?" and then gave him the raspberry. "You mean cheaper, don't you?"

His scowl deepened, which gave her a sense of satisfaction. Teasing this jerk was kind of entertaining.

She lifted her hand to signal a waitress. When she appeared, Caroline ordered another mezcal. Both the waitress and Victor raised their eyebrows. So what? *This night is going to be a nightmare, I might as well stick this lunatic with a hefty check.*

After the waitress walked away toward the bar, he quietly said, "I don't think you should have another one. Don't you have to drive home?"

"There's always Uber." She slurred her words, hiccupped, and then said, "Oh my God. I can't Uber home. I don't have any money."

CHAPTER TEN

The ringing phone startled her awake to a throbbing head that felt three times its normal size.

"Caroline, it's Michael. Did I wake you?"

His voice sounded so chipper she wanted to hang up. "Yes. What time is it and what do you want?"

"I was hoping you'd let me take you out for breakfast." Michael added, "I can pick you up."

Breakfast? A free breakfast. A real breakfast might be just what her head and her stomach needed after over-indulging the night before. Caroline wasn't sure she could get herself together in time for breakfast. "How about brunch? I'm not feeling too good this morning."

"Sure. I'll be there in an hour," he said and clicked off.

"Great. One hour," Caroline grumbled as she flung off the bed linens and stumbled to the bathroom.

True to his word, Michael picked her up punctually. She managed to shower and dress simply in her favorite pair of jeans, a Chanel tee shirt, and her Gucci tennis shoes.

She got into his car and fastened her seatbelt. "Where are we going?"

"You'll see." He put his Subaru Forester in gear, and they sped down the street.

Five minutes later, and two blocks over, they entered the diner.

Caroline's eyes shifted all around the classic 50s diner. Chrome and Formica everywhere, sunlight streaming through big plate glass windows. Two ibuprofen taken earlier had harnessed her pain, so the sunlight didn't bother her eyes as much. Still, she didn't remove her sunglasses. "I've never been here. Passed by hundreds of times."

Michael sat in the nearest empty booth. "It's delicious. Great food any time of the day or night."

Caroline slid onto the bench across from him. Picking up the menu, she said to the waitress, "Looks interesting. I'll have the egg-white western omelet, no home fries, and a coffee."

Michael ordered eggs benedict with home fries, bacon, and coffee.

"So what's the occasion?" Caroline added creamer to her coffee and took a sip. "Mm, good and hot."

"I was tired of telephoning. I thought it might be easier if we met." He waved his arm to encompass the entire seating area. "And here we are."

Caroline gave him a dubious look. "Right. It's eleven thirty. This must be your second breakfast?"

He shrugged. "What can I say? Breakfast is my favorite meal of the day. I'm not opposed to having it multiple times a day."

"What are you really up to?" Her eyes narrowed as she watched him. Something felt different.

"I wanted to see you. How did your date go last night?"

Caroline held up her palm. "Stop. I'm not discussing it."

Michael mashed his lips together and nodded. "Okay. How's the money holding out?"

"Not bad. I had to spend forty dollars last night for a ride home."

One of his eyebrows rose quizzically. "Okay. I won't ask about that either."

"Good."

The arrival of their food provided a brief respite, and Caroline savored a bite of her omelet.

"I reached a deal with the auto broker. The sale of the three cars will net you about a thousand over the balances due. Not too shabby."

She nodded before sipping her coffee. "The Jag, the Astin Martin, and the Hummer?"

"Yes." He meticulously spread the hollandaise sauce over his eggs, home fries, and bacon. "Any news from the real estate agent?"

QUEST FOR LOVE

Caroline looked at her plate as she set her fork down. "I forgot to call."

Michael's face grew drawn. His eyes closed as if he were in pain. "Caroline—"

She held up her hand again. "Stop. I forgot. I'll do it first thing this afternoon."

Thankfully for her, Michael changed the discussion topic.

"You'll have to find a place to live that's very inexpensive. When you find a place, I'll try to talk the landlord into reducing the security deposit."

A wide smile crept over her face. "I'm ahead of you there. My brother's condo might be available. If it is, he said I can stay there temporarily." Michael paused in his chewing as if waiting to hear something else. Caroline sighed. "For free."

"Excellent news!" He wiped his mouth with his napkin, his plate empty of contents.

"You ate all that all ready?" Caroline said, comparing his empty plate to her barely touched food.

"I've an appointment in an hour. Eat up, and I'll drop you off at home."

"I'm finished." She gave him her quizzical look. "Have I passed muster this morning?"

"One last question. Any luck finding a job?"

"Maybe. I'll let you know."

He grinned, "Great. Don't forget to call the agent." He handed the waitress cash for their bill and stood up. "Let's go."

Back at home, Caroline texted Regina.

> Hey, if your part-time job offer still stands, I'd like to try it out.

She waited for a reply, holding her head as she expected her brains to fall out of her eye sockets. Last night was a nightmare. What did she ever see in that guy? His profile sounded good. Victor hadn't sounded like a cheapskate. But he also hadn't sounded his age. She managed to get his real age out of him along with his occupation as a self-employed carpenter.

Over the remainder of their disastrous dinner of a taco salad shared between them, he'd bragged about high balling his customers, charging them four times his cost. Caroline never found out what he did with the money he earned. Cayman Islands? Not likely. The man didn't like to travel and had never set foot beyond the borders of the good old US of A.

He also let slip he'd previously been married before proceeding to tell her how he had managed to get the divorce judge to nix her request for support. As soon as his wife served him with divorce papers, he canceled half his customer projects so his income would be below his wife's. Then he pleaded, unsuccessfully, that she should pay him alimony.

In the end, the guy had nearly stroked out over the dinner check. Throwing down his napkin, he paid with his credit card and walked out. Caroline sat drunk, bemused, and alone. It was a crappy date, but the look on Victor's face had satisfied her. It was worth it. Except now she couldn't drive home. *Call Tony? Or call Rachel? Or wait for the alcohol to wear off?* She chose the latter, hanging out at the bar drinking water. At closing time, the hostess called an Uber to drive her home.

Her phone dinged that a notification had arrived. It was from Regina.

> Sure, you can start tomorrow if you'd like. Come by the shop at 10 a.m.

QUEST FOR LOVE

With that settled, Caroline rummaged through her walk-in closet, looking for something to wear. This no-money business was slowly ruining her life. She had another date tonight and had nothing clean to wear.

The pampered life she had grown up in didn't include many routine life skills. She'd watched the servants pick up her dirty clothes and return them clean and pressed the next day. The cook had shooed her from the kitchen by the time she was ten, and she'd never developed any interest in cooking on her own. Her fridge held a few Greek yogurt, sugar-free tea, and bottles of white wine.

The freezer section held one more Ben & Jerry's ice cream pint, one last frozen dinner, and a liter of vodka.

Nibbling on a saltine cracker, she considered asking Regina to teach her how to cook. Regina wasn't a gourmet cook but knew how to make a good meal. It wasn't Osso Bucco or shrimp scampi, but her food was filling and healthy. Perhaps she would give her a lesson. And teach her how to run a washer and dryer in her townhouse. Only the maid had ever used it.

Caroline picked up the cell phone again.

> Would you be willing to teach me how to cook simple meals? And how to do laundry?

Regina replied:

> I'm free today. Shall I come over in an hour? What do you know how to do already?

Caroline typed:

> Yes, please. Today is perfect. I know how to boil water for tea in the microwave.

Regina typed back:

> I was worried I'd have to teach you everything. LOL

CHAPTER ELEVEN

Regina arrived at Caroline's townhouse after one o'clock for Caroline's cooking and laundry lessons, toting two reusable grocery bags. "Wow, nice place." She admired the oversized living room with its thirty-foot wall of windows overlooking the Winooski River valley. The white monochrome walls, carpets, and furniture made her think of the all-white backdrops usually seen in depictions of heaven. The only splash of color was a cubist painting on the far wall.

"This way," Caroline said, leading her to the room on the right.

"I'm glad you already know how to boil water. That's a help," Regina said, walking into the expansive white marbled kitchen. It might have been immaculate when Caroline had a maid, but it was clear her sister-in-law also needed instructions on how to clean up and wash dishes. The trash can was overflowing. Stacks of dirty dishes, bowls, glasses, and mugs filled the five-foot-long counter beside the triple-basin kitchen sink. "I thought you didn't cook." Regina gestured toward all the plates and bowls.

"I don't. I've been using up the leftover meals from the freezer."

Hands on her hips, Regina turned to Caroline, "Well then, it looks like we need to do some clean up before we can start cooking."

Scrunching up her face, Caroline shrugged one shoulder. "Yeah. I'm useless in the kitchen. The maid does everything for me. Or she did until I had to let her go."

Setting her handbag on the nearest chair, Regina rolled up her sleeves. "Have you ever washed dishes before?" Regina stopped before the dishwasher. "You have a dishwasher."

Again, Caroline gave a lopsided grin and a shoulder shrug. "I have no idea how it works."

"Easy-peasy. Let's have a look." In less than a minute, Regina had figured it out. She opened the door. "First thing you have to do is empty out the clean dishes."

"How do I do that? The daily maid took care of the dishes, as well as the laundry and the cleaning. Once in a while, I had her make a pot of soup or roast a chicken." A blush stole up Caroline's cheeks. "I'm sorry, I don't remember where everything is supposed to go."

How was that even possible? Regina bit her lip to keep in the snarky comment. She opened the dishwasher door and then pulled out the upper rack. "Surely you know where the glasses and mugs go?"

Her lips tightened together, and tears threatening, Caroline nodded. She pointed to the two cabinets closest to the refrigerator.

"Well then, I'll pass them to you, and you can put them away. Yes?" Regina's head cocked slightly as she waited for a reply.

It took ten minutes to empty the dishwasher. Caroline could only guess where some of the things went. In the end, they had put away the things that Caroline could and then threw open all the cabinets to find out where the last items might reside.

"Now, let's fill her back up with these dirty things." Regina handed Caroline two dirty coffee mugs. "Glasses, mugs, and plastic wares in the upper rack. Plates, pans and almost everything else in the lower rack. When you're finished, add the soap to this compartment here, close it, press the Normal button, and then Start." She looked at the counter full of dirty dishes. "It might require two separate loads."

"Got it," Caroline said as she started to refill the machine. "It sounds easy when you explain it."

"Good. Where's your washer and dryer? I'll see if I can figure out how to operate them."

Caroline pointed down the hall. "Second door on the left. Behind the bi-fold doors." Regina watched Caroline fill up the dishwasher. It only held half of the dirty dishes on the counter. "Two loads it is," she muttered under her breath as she walked away.

A couple of minutes later, Regina poked her head out the utility room door. "Come on down and bring your dirty laundry."

QUEST FOR LOVE

Caroline detoured into her bedroom and emerged with an overloaded bin. Dragging the heaping laundry bin down the carpeted hallway, Regina met her at the door.

"First things first. You separate the clothes into four piles: whites that need bleach, those that don't, light-colored clothes and dark colored clothing." Regina pulled one of each item out of the bin and dropped it on the hallway carpet. "Like so."

It was obvious that Caroline still had no idea. "Can you help?" She held up a garment for Regina's response.

"Jeans all go in darks unless they are white or light colored."

It took twenty minutes before they had emptied the dirty laundry bin. Fortunately, Regina was able to mitigate a few disasters. The bright red blouse was placed in its own pile for separate washing, while the cashmere sweater and a few dresses were placed in a hand wash pile and dry-cleaning pile, respectively.

"This is so confusing." Caroline slumped against the wall.

"You'll get the hang of it." Arms crossed over her chest, Regina said, "Let's get a load started."

While Regina gave directions, Caroline filled the front loading washer and selected the program, water temperature, and spin speed. Next, Caroline added the laundry detergent to the dispenser under Regina's careful instruction and watchful eye.

"Okay. Press the Start icon, and we'll come back when it's finished to dry everything. Ready to start a cooking lesson?"

Caroline looked at Regina like she was about to fall over. "How about a short break? I'm exhausted."

"Sure thing. Let's take a few minutes to re-group." Regina headed back to the kitchen, with Caroline following on her heels.

Caroline bumped into Regina's backside when she stopped abruptly.

"Oh my God," Regina said, her hand covering her mouth.

"What? What's happened?" Caroline edged up to stand beside Regina at the entrance to the kitchen.

The floor was two feet deep in fluffy white soap bubbles.

"What the—?" Bubbles ejected from the dishwasher, some floating upward before either popping or falling back to join the thousands covering the white marble floor.

Regina's eyes were riveted on hers. "What soap did you use?"

Caroline's eyebrows came together. "The dishwashing soap. Why?"

Regina pointed at the blue liquid in the bottle beside the sink. "That one?"

"Yeah, why?"

Regina rolled her eyes and then closed them. She muttered, counting from one to ten. "That's not dishwasher *machine* soap. That's for hand-washing dishes in the sink." She gestured around the kitchen. "That's why there are soap bubbles everywhere."

She pulled out her cell phone and dialed. "Tony? Do you have a wet vac?" She paused as he replied. "Great, bring it over to your sister's townhouse. We've had a little mishap in the kitchen."

He arrived thirty minutes later with a small vacuum in hand. One look at the bubble mess had him slapping his hand over his mouth to stifle his laughter.

"Can it, Tony. It's been a trying day," Caroline snarled.

Her brother composed himself long enough to get to work with the vacuum. It didn't take long for him to suck up the mess while Regina and Caroline did more laundry.

When he finished, he took the trash to the dumpster and helped Caroline fold towels as Regina had instructed. "I heard back from the rental office. My condo will be empty in a few days. You can move in immediately."

Caroline flung her arms around him and hugged him tight. "Thank you, I'm sorry to impose, but I'm ever so grateful for this. I'll be out as soon as I can." She gave him a peck on his cheek. "Can I ask you for one more small favor?"

He glared at her, then at Regina, a glint of suspicion in his eyes. "What is it now?"

Regina mouthed, "Don't look at me."

Caroline asked, "Can you drive me over to the Mexican restaurant to pick up my car?"

A stunned look spread over his face. "What did you do?"

"Nothing. I had one too many to drive home, so I got a ride."

"That bad?" He eyed her again. At her one shoulder shrug, he asked, "What happened?"

Caroline rolled her eyes and shook her head. "Don't ask."

CHAPTER TWELVE

Teetering on her four-inch heels, Caroline walked across the parking lot behind the building that housed Gina Blooms. The old, chewed-up pavement would have been impossible to play the Crack Game she had learned at her private grammar school. The one where you're not supposed to step on any sidewalk cracks. She gingerly tiptoed, intent on keeping her pencil-thin heels from sinking into a crack and getting stuck. Or worse, damaging her Jimmys.

Her stomach growled. She'd had her kefir and fruit smoothie this morning, but it was past lunch time now. Maybe she should have picked up lunch at Jam Bakery? She took the stairs to the landing outside the door labeled Gina Blooms and rapped her knuckles on it to not further damage her week-old manicure. There was no telling when she'd be able to afford another. At one hundred and forty-five dollars a week, it wasn't going to happen any time soon. Neither was her weekly pedicure at one sixty a week. Of all the pampering she treated herself to, it was the weekly massages and facials she missed the most. Her face went hot thinking of the reactions of her masseuse and aesthetician when she called to cancel her standing appointments. Of course, she hadn't actually told them the truth. Rather, she'd said she had to visit her sick aunt. They had no idea she didn't have an aunt.

She glanced down at her dress and tried to smooth out the wrinkles that developed under the seat belts. The yellow A-line silhouette by Vera Wang revealed all her curves. Or her assets, as she liked to think of them. They were even more important now that she was active on the marriage market.

The door flung open, forcing Caroline to step aside rapidly. Regina stood framed in the doorway with a pair of scissors and a tulip in her free hand.

"Caroline!" Regina's eyes roamed over her from head to toe.

"I'm here to start work." She shrugged, her body gathering up tight like a turtle retreating into its shell under Regina's scrutiny.

Regina glanced at her watch. "I thought we agreed on ten this morning."

"I—I had trouble deciding what to wear."

"Next time, you might want to wear more sensible shoes. Something like ballet flats that won't kill your feet."

Caroline nodded without saying a word as the heat of a blush rose up her neck into her face. "If today's not good, I can come another day."

Regina said nothing as she stepped back to let her enter.

The dark interior of what was obviously some kind of storage room created shadows as it extended deep into the corners. Only a single fluorescent lamp hung from the old-fashioned tin ceiling. It cast its light onto two eight-foot-long stainless steel tables. One table was clean, and the other looked to be in the middle of a floral explosion. "I'm creating a birthday bouquet that needs to be delivered today." Regina glanced at her watch again. "The delivery truck should be here in half an hour."

"If today's not good—" Caroline injected again, feeling a little peeved at Regina's lack of warmth. Shouldn't her sister-in-law be happy to see her? Maybe her job offer had been one of those niceties one really didn't truthfully mean. Perplexed, Caroline bit back the rest of her statement.

"No, but I will set you up with my assistant for a little while." Regina put the scissors and tulip on the work table. She looked back at Caroline's outfit, taking it in head to toe again. Sighing, she said, "There's an apron on the wall behind you. I'd hate for your dress to become stained or ruined."

Caroline said nothing as she picked a green duck cloth apron off the wall hook and hung her purse in its place. She hadn't failed to notice Regina's attire consisted of a simple, black pencil skirt and a vibrant floral blouse beneath her own apron. Her black ballet flat shoes were covered with bits of flower petals. *At least she practices what she preaches.*

"So, this is the back room where all the floral designing happens. These refrigerated cabinets contain arrangements that will be delivered today." She pointed to the two largest cases behind the worktable. Then she turned to the nearest case. "This one contains all the different flowers and plant materials I stock for making the arrangements."

Regina waved for her to follow as she parted a green velvet curtain over a door frame. Light flashed through the slit in the curtain, partially blinding Caroline for a few seconds. As she walked through, she saw they were in the sales room.

To the right of the doorway was a tall counter holding a phone and a small rack of note cards to attach to arrangements. On a tall bar-type stool behind the counter, an older, woman, her silver-gray hair pulled back into a neat bun, sat before a computer screen.

The woman turned as Regina approached. "Another online order for the funeral tomorrow." She held out a slip of paper for Regina to take.

"Okay." Regina glanced at Caroline before returning her gaze to the woman. "This is Maggie, my assistant. Maggie, this is Caroline, Tony's sister. She's going to be working here part-time for a little while."

Surprise washed over Maggie's face. After a brief, awkward pause, Maggie held out her hand for a handshake. "Nice to meet you, Caroline."

Caroline grasped the tips of Maggie's fingers and gave them a little squeeze instead of a shake.

Maggie retracted her hand with a tentative smile on her face. She pushed a stray lock of her hair out of her eyes and stared at Caroline as if trying to assess her.

Regina interrupted their silent appraisal of each other. "Maggie, could you set Caroline up doing something? Watering the indoor plants, maybe? Or sweeping? Whatever you haven't had a chance to do yet."

"Sure thing." Maggie cocked her head to indicate Caroline should follow her out as she started for the front door.

Maggie led Caroline outside to the sidewalk, where a stand of buckets held bunches of cheerful flowers and bright bouquets. Pulling an empty bucket from behind the stand, she held it out to Caroline.

Caroline didn't like the looks of the dirty bucket, both inside and out. She held the wire handle between her thumb and index finger as far away from her dress as possible.

Her eyes blinking rapidly, Maggie said, "Okay. You need to inspect the flowers in each bucket. Remove any dying or dead leaves or blossoms. Like so." She demonstrated pinching off a browning leaf from a bunch of daisies and dropped it in the bucket. She pointed to a drooping bunch of tulips. "If you see drooping flowers, check to see if the bucket needs water. Make sure all the stems are in the water." She gently pushed the stems aside and peered inside. Grabbing a watering can from behind the stand, she added fresh water and returned the flower container to the stand. "Double-check this container in about half an hour to see if the flower heads have straightened up. Any questions?"

Caroline surveyed the entire rack. There were dozens of flower buckets. "I think I've got it."

With a nod, Maggie said, "Let me know if you have any problems or questions." She gave her a smile before returning inside the florist shop.

After assessing the entire rack, Caroline set down the empty bucket and began. Starting with the top tier, she went through each bucket. There weren't many bad leaves to remove, but when she did find one, she pinched it between her thumb and index finger, walked the offending plant material over to the bucket, and dropped it inside.

Some of the bouquets looked a little droopy, so she checked the containers for the water level, adding some as needed.

She was almost finished when, in the process of peering at the water level in a bucket, the heel of her shoe caught in a sidewalk crack. Off balance, she wobbled, trying to pull it out. Reaching out to steady herself, she grasped the stand. The next moment, she lay on the sidewalk under the toppled stand, staring up at the bright sky. Soaked with all the water from the buckets and surrounded by crushed and broken flowers, she called out for help.

The front door flung open, and Maggie rushed out. "Oh my, are you okay? What happened?" Maggie tried to lift the stand but couldn't do it alone. "Hold tight. I have to get help." She ran into the shop and returned with Regina.

Regina stopped in her tracks, eyes widened and mouth hanging open. "Oh, Caroline, are you okay?"

"I'm soaking wet. My silk dress—my shoes—" Hot tears filled her eyes as she realized everything she wore was ruined. Her expression crumpled as she also realized bystanders on the opposite sidewalk were staring at her disastrous predicament.

The two women righted the stand and helped Caroline to her feet, but her shoe remained stuck in the sidewalk crack. Caroline wiggled her foot to loosen it, but it wouldn't budge. Finally, she yanked hard. The heel broke off, while the rest of the shoe came free. Caroline groaned again but ignored the heel wedged in the sidewalk crack. Regina and Maggie surveyed the pile of dripping and empty buckets, the scattered bouquets and flowers crumpled by the weight of the metal stand.

"I—I'm going home." Caroline sniffled, wiping her eyes with the backs of her hands as she limped back into the store to retrieve her purse.

QUEST FOR LOVE

On the way home, she considered canceling tonight's date. Not wanting to revive Michael's ire, she decided a nap would suffice before getting ready for her next date.

CHAPTER THIRTEEN

Thick cucumber slices slid down her face and dropped onto her naked chest when she sat up. Caroline wiped her eyes with the backs of her hands before blinking several times. A glance at the bedside clock made her start.

"Oh shit." Jumping out of bed, she ran to the bathroom to run the water. She was due to meet tonight's date in forty minutes at a restaurant twenty minutes away. *You should have taken a shower before taking your nap.*

She lathered up with the lavender and chamomile soap and rinsed just as quickly with the hand wand. A quick spritz of perfume, and then she slapped on some moisturizer and body lotion. Throwing open the walk-in closet doors, she searched for something appropriate to wear. It took several passes through the thirty-foot line of clothing to decide on a Madras skirt and peasant blouse. Glancing in the mirror, she noted her eyes still looked a little swollen. There was no help for it at this point. She didn't have the luxury of time. Another glance at the clock indicated she had only a few minutes to get in the car. Otherwise, she would be late for this date.

The guy she was meeting tonight sounded like a promising marriage candidate. A lawyer out of Brattleboro, he planned to meet her at Delaney Tavern, a local watering hole in nearby Windsor. At thirty-five, he said he had never married and was ready to settle down. He liked to travel, ski in the winter, boat in the summer, and lived in an old Victorian house close to the main street in Wilmington.

By the time Caroline arrived, she was five minutes late. She should have gotten there in plenty of time, driving her favorite car, a powder blue vintage Mustang. But a lumbering tractor-trailer truck had turned into her path from a highway exit ramp.

When she pulled in, Daryl was pacing the parking lot, waiting for her. His frown overshadowed the European cut of his dress trousers and crisp white button-down shirt. As she got out of the car, he approached. "I was beginning to think I was stood up," he said, slamming her car door when she was clear. *At least this guy knows how to dress more appropriately.*

"No. I wouldn't do that. A slow-moving truck got in front of me. There wasn't any way to pass it on the back roads."

Inside the tavern, they were seated at a white linen-clad table not far from the kitchen's swinging doors. They ordered drinks: a martini for Daryl and a Pinot Grigio for Caroline. She would have to control her drinking tonight. The last thing she wanted was to get too drunk to drive herself home again.

When the drinks were delivered, they ordered fried calamari for an appetizer. Daryl ordered a steak, while Caroline chose chicken marsala.

"So, tell me about your work," Caroline suggested. "What kind of law practice do you do? Real estate?"

Daryl scoffed. "I'm a bankruptcy attorney."

Caroline's insides twisted in a knot as she nodded. "That must be hard. Trying to help out people who have fallen on hard times."

"Actually, it's rather comical. So many people can't seem to live within their means. I don't feel sorry for the lot of them."

Feeling uneasy in her stomach. If he only knew she was one of those people. Caroline asked, "What about people who are sick? Who can't afford health care?"

He frowned. "Yes, there are a lot of them. So many of them live so poorly, with poor nutrition, they smoke, they drink too much. It's hardly a wonder why they get so sick. Let's face it, some people are asking for it."

The unease in her gut was starting to blossom. This man was as uncompassionate as they came. Time to change the subject. "Do you do any pro bono work?"

"Nah. There's always someone looking for a free hand-out. People always come into the office looking for someone to handle their cases for free. Nobody gave me a free law education. I had to pay for it on my own."

He must have seen the horrified expression on her face. "There are other lawyers in the group that do that kind of shit. I can't be bothered. It's been my experience that the clients don't appreciate it." He snapped up a large fried calamari, dipped it in the marinara sauce, bit half of it, then -double-dipped it before popping the rest into his mouth. "They often come back repeatedly, looking for more free representation for all sorts of other problems." He used air quotes when saying 'problems,' his fingers smeared with grease and marinara sauce.

Caroline stirred uncomfortably in her seat. The waitress brought their dinners. Caroline was grateful for something to concentrate on, and hoped Daryl would keep his mouth shut except for chewing. His comments were rubbing her the wrong way. She might be a trust-fund baby, but she still had some compassion in her soul for those who genuinely needed legal assistance for reasons beyond their control.

Daryl picked a piece of parsley off his plate and threw it aside. "Stupid garnish. I can't stand parsley."

Caroline chose to ignore his mutterings. Her meal was hot and it looked and smelled earthy from the mushroom-laden marsala sauce.

He cut a huge piece of steak from the center, glared at it, and waved the waitress back. "It's overdone. I asked for medium rare. This," he held up his fork to just under her nose, "this is medium."

The waitress, who had stepped back from the fork, rolled her eyes, picked up his plate, and shuffled back to the kitchen without saying a word.

Caroline chose to keep eating. Her meal was fine. She suspected his steak had been fine also, but he was trying to impress her. Little did he know his antics made her wish this date could be over.

He eyed her as she continued eating, a begrudging look on his face. "How's your dinner? Cooked to your liking?"

QUEST FOR LOVE

Having just placed a chunk of meat in her mouth, Caroline took her dear sweet time chewing before swallowing. "Mine is fine. Delicious, in fact."

The waitress brought a new steak back. "Here you are, sir. This should be better." The woman stood aside, waiting for his approval. She didn't have to wait long for his response.

Daryl cut the steak in half in the middle and eyed it suspiciously. "It's still overdone." He picked up the plate and shoved it back at the waitress.

Caroline saw the barely hidden smirk on the waitress's face before she exited with the plate again. She leaned forward. "I thought that looked fine."

Daryl glared at her. "These people don't give a shit. I don't know why I come here. It happens every time." He drained his martini and held up his empty glass to a passing waiter, who promptly turned away to ignore him. A growl came across the table. "Insolence. Damn immigrants are all alike."

Caroline inhaled sharply. On the one hand, she was glad to learn this man's true colors. On the other hand, his behavior was embarrassing, and she was becoming increasingly aware of her gut telling her to get up and leave this idiot. Not to mention the stares of the other restaurant patrons. While Daryl might have a handsome face and wear tailor-cut fashion, his attitude and behavior severely detracted from whatever it was that had initially attracted her to him on the website.

The waitress arrived again and set a silver-dome-covered plate before him. "I think this one will be rare enough to suit you." With a flourish, she snatched off the dome and briskly walked away.

Both Daryl and Caroline stared at the plate. A raw steak filled the plate. Daryl slammed down his napkin and stood so abruptly his chair clattered to the floor. He scooped up the plate and stalked toward the kitchen door, his face thunderous with rage.

Caroline watched as he disappeared behind the door. A fury of screaming and yelling erupted from the kitchen. The waitress came running out screaming, "Call the police." Everyone in the restaurant turned to stare at the kitchen door and then at Caroline as if she had something to do with the situation. She gave the other patrons a shrug and took a last sip of wine. She wiped her mouth, grabbed her purse, and left Daryl to deal with the situation he had created. And the check.

CHAPTER FOURTEEN

At Regina's insistence, Caroline arrived for another attempt at the part-time job. This time, she wore something simpler and less costly. The black ballet flats, black cigarette pants, crisp, white short-sleeved blouse, and the colorful silk scarf around her neck flattered her petite figure and comfortably fit her. Caroline thought the outfit gave her a chic, Parisian flair.

She arrived for her job at noon. This time, she entered through the shop's front door, being careful not to interrupt or break Maggie's focus as she took an in-person order from a client. Caroline slipped through the green velvet curtains into the back room.

"There you are. I was beginning to think you changed your mind about giving it another try." Regina was putting a new arrangement into the cooler.

Caroline tried to smile. "I considered it. But I thought after yesterday's disaster, I deserved another try." She hung up her purse and donned the shop apron. "I couldn't decide what to wear."

Regina placed a hand on her upper arms and looked Caroline in the eyes. "We did agree on a ten o'clock start. When you have a job, it's important that you arrive at the appointed time."

Her eyes widened. "I'm sorry. I guess I have a lot to learn about being an employee."

Reaching her arm around Caroline's shoulder, Regina nodded. "It's okay. I know you have never worked. These are all lessons every person learns." She smiled before adding, "Usually around the age of sixteen."

"I never expected to need a job."

"I know. It's probably a good thing you're with me for your first." Regina gave her a wink. She reached behind her and thrust a broom into her hands. "First task today is to sweep this back room floor and the salesroom floor. But you have to be very careful not to knock anything over."

Caroline shook her head. "I'm never going to live down that incident, am I?"

Grinning wide, Regina said, "Nope. Consider yourself lucky I didn't have my camera with me."

Giggling, Caroline rolled her eyes and covered her throat with her hand. "I must have looked pretty funny soaking wet."

"Oh! You have no idea!" Regina chuckled and strode off in the direction of the salesroom.

The broom in hand, Caroline began sweeping. It wasn't something she had ever done before. She had seen it done by the maids, housekeeper, and even the cook at her parents' homes while growing up. It didn't take her long to figure out how to work it, though she did have a little trouble watching where she was walking. Sometimes, she would create a small pile of plant debris only to accidentally kick it, re-spreading it across the floor.

Regina came back just as she finished creating yet another pile.

"How do I pick it up?" Caroline asked, her mind a little fuzzy on that part of the task. She couldn't remember ever having seen that part.

"There's a dustpan hanging on the wall over there." Regina pointed to a spot near the shelving units.

Caroline retrieved the pan and attempted to leave it lying on the floor and sweep the pile into it. Except it kept moving when the broom's bristles hit it.

Regina stepped forward. "Let me show you." With the broom in her right hand and the pan in her left, Regina bent down and swept up the pile of plant and product detritus.

"Oh, got it," Caroline said, her hands out to take the broom and pan back. Once equipped again, she finished the task in minutes.

"Great job. Thank you. Did you do the sales room, too?"

Caroline rolled her eyes. "Sorry, I forgot." She stepped through the curtain. Starting at the front of the store, she wielded the broom as best she could. The floor space was filled with potted plants, plant stands,

QUEST FOR LOVE

and shelves of goods either made from botanicals or decorated with them. Getting under the stands and shelving proved challenging. The broom's wooden handle slipped in her sweating palms. She adjusted her grip several times as she viewed a wrought iron stand filled with pots of blooming orchids. The variety of colors and sizes displayed were interesting.

"There you are! How's it going?" Maggie called out.

Startled, Caroline spun around to see who had spoken to her. Her abrupt turn sent the broom flying. It struck the stand of orchids, sending the potted plants in every direction. "Oh no!" She tried to catch a few pots as they tumbled to the floor but only caught hold of the plants themselves. The delicate blossoms ripped off their stems, crushed in her hands as the pots shattered and potting soil spilled across the hardwood flooring. Closing her eyes, she prayed that when she opened them, it would just be a bad nightmare.

It wasn't a nightmare. She burst into tears, humiliated at her clumsiness and stupidity.

When she dared to look up, Maggie's face was filled with shock, and Regina grimaced, her jaw tense, her teeth clenched.

"I'm so sorry I scared you," Maggie said, reaching for the fallen broom. "I'll clean it up."

Unable to say anything coherent, Caroline let Regina steer her into the back room, with her hand tightly gripping Caroline's forearm. She steeled herself for what she knew was coming—getting fired.

Behind the green velvet curtain, Regina released her arm but kept walking to the back wall of the room, her palm cradling her forehead. She stayed like that as if turned to stone.

Neither of them said anything for a few minutes.

With each second, Caroline's mood sank deeper until she couldn't stand the silence any longer. Between her tears, she muttered to Regina's back, "I'm so sorry. She scared me." When Regina remained still, she added, "I know. I'm fired." Her tears came harder now. "I'll just leave."

Her sister-in-law visibly inhaled deeply and exhaled forcefully before turning around. Deep lines etched Regina's face, revealing the agony she was feeling. "You need a break to calm down. Can you walk down to Jam Bakery and pick up my order and Maggie's? I called it in ten minutes ago. While you're there, order yourself something. Have them put your purchase on my tab."

Nodding, Caroline wiped her eyes and stepped out the shop's back door.

CHAPTER FIFTEEN

The inside of Jam Bakery looked very different from the last time Caroline had been there. Gone were the multicolored tiles in a harlequin pattern. The walls were now glossy cream, the trim and shelving behind the counter painted bright yellow. It gave the entire space a bright, warm feel. The sales counter and dining area looked even bigger with the new decor. Potted houseplants still hung in front of the large pane picture window. Samples of today's baked items were displayed on colorfully patterned plates, each with a clear glass dust cover. The sight made everyone stop to look at the goodies being offered. Fifty percent, mainly tourists, stepped through the door for a purchase.

Caroline approached the marble-topped counter to get a closer look at the menu. The mishap had tamped down her appetite. She wasn't hungry anymore but free food was free.

"Hey, Caroline, How are you? We haven't seen you in these parts in a while," Jamaica Jones said as she advanced toward the counter with a large bag of food that she set aside. "What can I get you?"

"A cup of the vegan chili and a brioche bun." She lowered her voice a little. "I'm also here to pick up Regina's order. She said you can add my order to the tab."

"Is yours to go also?" Jamaica smiled. When she saw Caroline shake her head, she pulled a brioche bun from the display case. "Excellent choices. I just brought this in from the kitchen." Turning her back to Caroline, she scooped a large ladle of chili into a bowl.

Caroline's heart thumped. "Just a cup, Jamaica. Please."

Jamaica's grin broadened. "You look like you've lost a lot of weight. You need a full bowl of my chili."

Caroline nodded her thanks as the bag of food was passed to her.

"You go find a seat, and I'll bring the tray over for you." Jamaica inclined her head in the direction of the dining area and followed Caroline to a small table near the front window.

"How's Ronnie and the baby?" Caroline asked. She didn't like small talk, but Jamaica had always been a friend. Her take-charge attitude but calm influence had always made Caroline feel special. Perhaps she did that with everyone. Either way, Caroline appreciated it. There weren't all that many people who made her feel comfortable anymore.

"Baby? Who told you?" Jamaica whispered. "I didn't think anybody knew yet."

Caroline could feel the shock on her own face. "I—I didn't know. I was talking about Willow."

Jamaica rolled her eyes. "I guess I let that out of the bag all by myself." She sat down in the chair opposite Caroline. "Don't say anything just yet. Ronnie knows, of course, but I haven't told my father and Mary yet."

A surprising warmth filled her chest. She was party to a secret. Perhaps the first one anyone had ever given her. "I won't tell a soul."

"Ronnie's over the moon. Willow's walking and jabbering away already. She'll be one in a few weeks." Jamaica rolled her eyes again. "If she would only sleep better at night, both Ronnie and I would be grateful."

"Still not sleeping the entire night?"

"Oh, she was, but now she's teething." Jamaica slumped back in her seat. "The entire household is in an uproar. Even Burpy."

"Burpy?" Caroline wasn't sure who this Burpy was.

"The stray dog Ronnie and I adopted after the hurricane. He nearly got me drowned."

Caroline gave a wide-eyed, exaggerated stare. "I'm not a fan of animals, though Regina's three cats are tolerable. But I certainly wouldn't be a fan if one almost drowned me."

Jamaica chuckled. "Too long a story." Jamaica waved her hand as if to dismiss the tale. "So what have you been up to, young lady?"

"Dating, and working for Regina. Or, I should say, trying to."

It was Jamaica's turn to look amazed. "You're working?"

Caroline gave a tense smile. "I've been there only two days, and I've managed to wreak havoc and mayhem on both occasions. Frankly, I think I'd have been fired already if I wasn't Regina's sister-in-law."

A hearty chuckle erupted from Jamaica. "So you're looking for another job?"

"I think I better. If only for familial peace." Caroline cringed. "I just don't know how to work. I've never had to, so I don't know about things like arriving on time and appropriate clothing. God only knows what else I've never had to learn to land and keep a job."

Jamaica stared at her thoughtfully for a half minute while Caroline spooned into her chili bowl. "I could use a part-timer this time of day to help clean up for closing."

Remembering her townhouse, Caroline shook her head as she chewed a bite of brioche. "I'm not good at cleaning up. Do you have anything else?"

The older woman thought another minute. "You could help Isabelle make jam. Have you ever made homemade jam before?"

"Never."

"Well, if you'd like, over the next two weeks, Isabelle will be here to make our supply of jams: strawberry, raspberry, cherry, and my personal favorite, Merry Berry. It's a mixture of all those berries and a few other fruits. It's delicious. I like to give out jars at Christmas time to my best customers."

The thought of making jam intrigued her. "Is it easy?"

"Relatively. You have to crush the fruit and boil it with sugar and pectin before canning it. It's hot work in the summer, but that's when the fruit is ripest and most delicious. In mid-summer, we'll make peach and then blueberry jam. Want to give it a try?"

Caroline hesitated. It sounded interesting. And taking Jamaica's job offer would get her out of Regina's hair. "Yes. I'll help."

"Good. I'll let Isabelle know she has a helper. First day is next Monday, about ten in the morning." One of the other staff waved for Jamaica to return to the kitchen. "It seems I'm being summoned. Enjoy your lunch." Jamaica disappeared behind the swinging doors.

Caroline finished her chili and brioche while lazily thumbing through all the messages sent to her dating page. As Jamaica returned from the register, a lovely, ethereal woman entered the bakery. "Elowen! Are you ready for the meeting tonight?"

The slim, strawberry blonde's delicate facial features and skin glowed despite her tired eyes. "Escaping the shop for a few minutes. If I'm going to last until closing at seven, I need some coffee and something for dinner."

Jamaica returned to the counter, taking the woman's order and handing over an extra-large coffee cup. Seeing Caroline staring, she brought Elowen over to meet Caroline. "Caroline Perret, this is Elowen Sparkle. She owns Sparkle Jewelry."

Caroline shook hands with the petite young woman. "I've always wanted to visit your shop, but I never seem to get there."

"I'd love to show it to you. Stop by anytime. I'm always there." Elowen turned to Jamaica. "Except tonight. I'll be at the Women's Business Alliance meeting at The Dockside this evening."

Jamaica lovingly placed her hands on Elowen's shoulders. "Miss Elowen is going to be voted in as the next president of the alliance."

"Wow, I've never heard of the alliance."

Jamaica said, "You should come along tonight if you're not busy. We're a fun group. Even when we get down to business."

Caroline nodded. "Okay. I'll go. I'm interested to see what it's all about."

A salesgirl approached, bringing Elowen's order wrapped in a paper bag.

QUEST FOR LOVE

"You're welcome to join me." Caroline gestured to the empty seat.

"I'd love to, but I have to get back. It's my one employee's last day, and she leaves in an hour."

Jamaica piped in, "Oh, right." She glanced from Elowen to Caroline. "If I hadn't already hired her, you could have hired Caroline. She's looking for work."

Elowen winked at Caroline. "If it doesn't work out here, come see me."

As Elowen exited onto the sidewalk, Caroline's cell phone rang. It was Regina. "Hello?"

Exasperation filled Regina's voice. "What is taking so long? Maggie and I are waiting for our lunch."

"You told me to get whatever I wanted." Caroline's tone was tight, like her face. Really, the woman was getting on her nerves.

"I didn't mean for you to stay there and eat it while our lunches get cold."

"I'm sorry. I didn't think." Caroline dropped her forehead into her palm. "I'll be right over with them. And consider this my last day." She blew out a puff of air, grabbed the bags, and headed down the street.

CHAPTER SIXTEEN

"Do you have a reservation?" the hostess asked Caroline when she entered the Dockside Restaurant.

"I'm here for the women's group." Caroline scanned the faces of people seated in the dining area. Jamaica and Elowen were not there.

"They are meeting in the event room. Walk through to the other side of the bar. You'll see them."

Caroline gave her a quick nod and followed the directions, finding the expansive room filled with women of every size, age, and ethnicity. Jamaica spotted her and waved her over to her table.

"You did come." She smiled, pulling out the empty chair beside her for Caroline.

"I can't believe all the women here. I didn't expect so many." Her eyes wandered the breadth of the room; many women she didn't know and a few she did. "Regina's here."

"She better be! She's our current president." Jamaica glanced at her watch. "But only for the next hour or so."

Caroline's heart beat faster. The sight of so many gathered together astounded her. "I had no idea there were so many businesswomen in Fulton River."

"Women outnumber male business owners in this town. There's another business alliance group called the Downtown Merchants Association. It used to be co-ed, but the men refused to share leadership, so we women started our own association." She grinned. "Elowen is expected to take over as president tonight."

"Who can join? Is it only business owners?"

Jamaica shook her head. "Any woman owning or working in a Fulton River business is welcome." She nudged Caroline's shoulder with her own. "Even you could join."

For the first time in her life, Caroline thought of being a woman business owner. Prior to that moment, all she knew was what her mother had told her. That a woman's purpose was to manage children, the household, and whatever necessary to support her husband's career. It had never occurred to her mother that she could have a life and career of her own. The possibility intrigued Caroline. A knocking of a gavel at the podium interrupted her thoughts.

Regina called out, "Order ladies. Let's get the business finished so we can eat and socialize." Regina's eyes locked on Caroline. "Wait, we have a guest tonight. Everyone, please welcome Caroline Perrett."

The crowd gave Caroline a hardy welcome that made her face get hot. Caroline hadn't expected Regina to acknowledge her at all. She had expected Regina to be angry at the havoc she'd caused. Those buckets of flowers and the orchids and their pots must have cost Regina a fortune to replace.

Regina gave her a wink and a smile before quieting everyone down and proceeding with the agenda.

The evening's meeting transpired quickly. Regina opened the floor for nominations for secretary, treasurer, vice president, and president. Within thirty minutes, the ballot counters announced the results.

"Elowen Sparkle is our new president, Carlotta Martinez is our new vice president, Stacey Tinker is secretary, and Florence Quinn is treasurer."

As the crowd clapped and hooted their endorsement, Jamaica leaned toward Caroline. "You should join."

A warmth filled Caroline's chest. She'd never been asked to join something that wasn't frivolous. She hoped the dues weren't so high that she couldn't afford them. "How much does it cost?"

Jamaica's smile widened. "It's free."

Caroline gave her an unbelieving glare.

"Seriously. It's free. You'll have to pay twenty dollars per meeting to cover the cost of food if you intend to eat." She gestured toward the back of the room to a long row of tables where food had been set up. "It's usually soups, salads, or platters of sandwich fixin's."

Realizing she hadn't thought to bring much money, Caroline cringed inside. "I don't think I have enough cash on me."

Jamaica waved away her concern. "You're my guest tonight. It's on me."

Regina walked up beside her and gave her a hug. "I didn't know you were coming."

"Jamaica invited me. I didn't know you were president!" Caroline kissed her cheek. "You never mentioned this group."

"You weren't a Fulton River businesswoman. Besides, I didn't think you'd be interested." Regina slipped her arm around Caroline's slim waist. "Stop by the shop and pick up your paycheck."

She couldn't believe her ears. "You're going to pay me for my two days of work, even after all the mess and damage I caused?"

"Of course. You did work, and you did help clean up your messes." Regina squeezed Caroline tight to her side. "You'll find your niche. It's going to take some time, but I believe you'll figure it out."

Caroline couldn't fathom how Regina would be so nice to her after all the mess and expense her mayhem had caused. Was it only because they were sisters-in-law? She didn't think so. Did Regina really care what happened to her? She remembered the cooking lesson, the laundry lesson, and—she cringed just thinking about it—the dishwasher incident. Yet Regina had still allowed her to work at her shop. The woman was either nuts, or she believed in her. The mere thought Regina was being so supportive made her get teary-eyed. It was more than some of her so-called friends had ever done.

CHAPTER SEVENTEEN

The following day, she stepped into the accountant's small office. The receptionist, Gabriella, sat at her desk. She gestured toward the empty chairs and disappeared into Michael's office.

Caroline sat beside the small table holding well-thumbed magazines. Seeing the latest Vogue, she glanced up at the door. Her own subscription had ended last month, and she hadn't had time to renew it. With her money situation now, she knew Michael would never allow it.

She spied if anyone was looking. While she watched the office door for Gabriella or Michael to come through it, she stuffed the magazine into her oversized bag. Hoping to look innocent, she sat back in the chair with her legs crossed. The leg perched on her knee bobbed to a tune blasting through her earbuds. Waiting tested her patience. She hated it. It reminded her of her childhood, hurrying off to what she had been told would be a trip to the ice cream parlor. Only to find out she had to sit through one of her father's campaign stops and behave like "a young lady of breeding."

She glanced over at the receptionist's desk. With so many picture frames crowded on the desktop around her computer screen and keyboard, Caroline couldn't see how the woman got anything done.

Michael had requested a check-in meeting to see what progress she had made to shore up her finances. She felt a little squeamish to tell him she hadn't done anything but go on two dates and quit her only job after two calamitous days.

Minutes later, the receptionist returned. "Mr. DuBois can see you now." She left the door open to the inner office. The darkly stained wainscot gave the room a dismal appearance. She shivered. She never liked this room. It reminded her of her father's library at the Fulton River house. It reminded her of what happened there.

"You need to redecorate. I can make some wonderful suggestions," Caroline offered as she entered the room.

"Another time. Come in, please, have a seat," Michael said, not looking up from his computer screens. His eyes darted back and forth between them as if he were surveying them. "Thank you for coming."

"I didn't realize I had an option not to come," she growled. "It felt like a court summons."

His blue eyes glared at her now. "It's always in your best interest to meet with me. Especially now."

She sat in the chair before his desk, dropped her purse on the empty seat beside her, and glared back at him. "Why is that?" She couldn't help the haughty tone of her voice. His words rubbed her like coarse sandpaper across the wood grain.

He frowned. "I didn't get you into this mess. You did. I'm trying to help you save your credit rating and your reputation."

She scowled. "Can you get to the point? I have a date tonight. In—" She glanced at her Rolex watch. "Forty-nine minutes."

"Right." A hint of a smile teased the corners of his mouth. "Have you found yourself a husband yet?"

"Still working on it, but the prospects are good. I've had lots of interest."

He steepled his fingers over his mouth. "So you'll be married in a few weeks?"

She stood and began pacing the room. "I said, I'm working on it."

"Good." Michael typed something into his computer, letting the clicking sound of the keyboard fill the silence between him and his client. "And have you spoken with the real estate agent? Listed the townhouse?"

"Why should I? I'm getting married in the next few weeks."

He frowned and shoved a letter across the desk at her. Her mortgage company's letterhead adorned the top. "You should, because of this."

QUEST FOR LOVE

Caroline stared at the letter but made no movement toward it. "What does it say?"

Michael entwined his fingers on the desktop and leaned forward. His head cocked as if he were reading the letter upside down. "I asked the mortgage company for a temporary hold on payments. As you might recall, the mortgage is automatically paid from your checking account. I also asked to suspend that automatic payment for a month. The letter is their reply."

Stopping by the window, she quirked one delicate eyebrow back at him.

"They declined to hold off on taking the next payment." He sat back in his black faux leather chair. "If they take the next payment out, there will not be enough money to pay your other creditors with the remaining balance." He stared at her as if she didn't understand. When she made no comment, he added, "You will be one giant step closer to having to declare bankruptcy."

Her mouth went dry. On wobbly knees, she sat down in her chair again. "What will happen?"

"The mortgage company evicts you from your townhouse. Your possessions may be repossessed by the sellers. Your remaining vehicles, the ones you own, will be seized, loaded on flatbed trucks, and taken away. In the meantime, we find a lawyer to fill out the paperwork. In a couple months, you'll go to bankruptcy court, and a judgment will be rendered."

Was that a glint of sadness in his eyes? "In my favor?"

"No. You will lose everything. Including your Mustang."

She sputtered, "But it was a gift! I own it. I just had it repainted after someone keyed it."

"The proceeds from its sale could be used to pay your creditors."

Tears welled so fiercely that Caroline closed her eyes, trying to prevent them from spilling down her face. She mashed her lips together.

"And then I can start over. The debts will be cleared, and I'll get my credit cards back?" She searched her purse for a handkerchief.

"I'm afraid your credit will be in shambles. You will lose all your credit cards. Not a bad thing, in my humble opinion." He cleared his throat before adding, "It will be up to ten years before you can use anything other than cash or check. For anything."

A lump the size of a watermelon filled her throat. This was bad. So bad. "What can I do?"

"First, you need to list that townhouse for sale. We can try for a quick sale. You need to move out, find someplace to live until it does."

Tears cascaded down her cheeks. "My brother's condo is empty. I'll be moving in there."

"Good. After you list the townhouse, you need to relinquish the vehicles. I'll get the auto dealer to finish the transfer paperwork pronto. It's better to give them back than have them repossessed. It will ding your credit rating, but far less than a hostile repossession."

"What about all my furniture, my jewelry, everything else?" She wailed, her handkerchief wet with tears.

"You'll have to sell some of it, like the jewelry. The rest can be put into storage until you're back on your feet enough to rent an apartment. Anything you bought on credit can be repossessed by the seller."

From the look on her face, her defiance was gone. In its place was defeat. Michael's heart ached for her. The severity of the situation was finally getting through. He hated being the one to make her face the facts. He wished his father was still alive to handle the situation. But he knew in his heart his father had been part of the problem all along. Giving Caroline chances, looking the other way as she spent and spent and spent. All with little serious warning, without making her face the ramifications of her diminishing financial situation. Michael glanced down at his hands, folded tightly on the desk. He would not let this situation kill him. Not like his father had.

"There's one more thing. You rented a house on Mount Desert Island in Maine for two weeks, starting the week after next. You paid in full. It's non-refundable even if you cancel. What do you want to do?"

Caroline's eyes were blank. The tears had stopped. But the anguish on her face, evident by the tightness of her lips, the set of her jaw, and the angle she held her head, spoke of her feelings. "Perhaps if I get lucky tonight, I might need it for a honeymoon."

CHAPTER EIGHTEEN

Standing outside Woohoo Burger joint, Caroline looked up and down the sidewalk. There wasn't anyone that looked like her date. Kyle was supposed to be twenty-five years old with blond hair and blue eyes, about six feet tall.

She glanced at her watch for the fifth time in ten minutes. He was late. She glanced up the street again while debating between waiting another five minutes or just calling this date over before it began.

No one fitting that description was walking toward her. Instead, she saw an older-looking man with white hair. As he approached, his eyes riveted onto hers and wouldn't let go. Four feet away from her, he grinned beneath his full beard and asked, "Are you Caroline? I'm Kyle." He had to be at least fifty.

Wasn't that dating site only for those under thirty? She could only stare at him. There was something about him that made her cringe. What was she going to do?

As if sensing her dismay, the man held out his right hand to shake hers. Still flabbergasted by the man's obvious age difference from what she was expecting, Caroline shook it. The grip sealed her fate for the evening. *Merciful God, please let this date be very short.*

Kyle grabbed the door handle, opening it for Caroline to pass into the fast food restaurant tucked into a narrow space. Still speechless, Caroline entered, sparks of creepy zipping all over her body as she felt him place his hand on her lower back as she passed him. A shudder rolled through her entire body like a tsunami. She stepped forward out of Kyle's reach just to get his hand off her.

The line to order at the counter started just inside the door. Kyle stepped in front of her in line as they shuffled forward without speaking until it was their turn to order.

QUEST FOR LOVE

"We'll each have a double bacon cheeseburger with ketchup, mustard, mayo, and relish. Add two large French fries and two diet Dr. Peppers."

Caroline found her voice and blurted, "That's not what I want. I'd like a turkey burger." Kyle turned his back to her as he handed over his credit card to pay for their meals. Noticing his indifference, she added, "I don't eat red meat, nor do I eat bacon or cheese. And I do not eat French fries."

Kyle glanced over his shoulder at her and gave her a single nod, indicating supposedly that he had heard her. But he made no move to change the order to suit her. He tucked his hand against the small of her back again and pushed her a little too forcibly. Caroline gave him a death glare, which he ignored, and picked out a table for two in a long row of identical tables along the far side of the room. Caroline sat, her hands clutching her purse in her lap. Her shoulders rigid and squared. The tension in her body acutely attuned to this man and his rude behavior.

"Well now, what shall we talk about?" Kyle asked, his eyes not meeting hers.

"I'd like to talk about the order you placed for me that I will not eat." As she said this, the restaurant staff delivered a tray filled with food. The woman set the tray on the table between them, glanced at Caroline, and walked back to the kitchen area. She caught the sympathetic look of the young man seated at the table behind Kyle.

Taking one of the wrapped double bacon cheeseburgers and one of the large French fry sleeves, he dove in. Kyle stuffed his mouth with a large bite of his burger. He grabbed a soda, placing it on the table beside his plate. He seemed undaunted that she refused to eat.

There had to be something wrong with this man that he could not and would not understand why she refused to eat the food he provided.

"You should eat what I bought for you," Kyle said before snatching a bunch of fries and shoving them into his mouth. The light flashed on a college ring. The graduation year on it was thirty-two years ago.

Caroline just glared at him, her hands still clenched in her lap. "If you like red meat so much, you can eat it for me."

"Don't mind if I do." Kyle reached for her wrapped burger on the tray. "I'm not going to let good food go to waste."

"So let me tell you a little bit about me," Kyle said between chewing on fries. He then proceeded to speak nonstop to Caroline, the entire time eating and disregarding the venomous stare she was sending.

When Kyle started talking about his love life, his ex-wife, and how she left him, Caroline decided that was enough. She wasn't going to listen to his pity party. The reasons his ex-wife left were clear. She wasn't going to put up with him either. She stood up.

Kyle gazed up at her with a fistful of fries. "Where are you going? To the ladies' room?"

"No, " she said, "I've had enough. Thank you for meeting with me. May I advise you next time you decide to solicit a date with someone online that you tell them your real age."

Kyle jumped up and threw his arm around Caroline's shoulders. He even puckered up in an attempt to kiss her. Revolted by his touch and his mouth full of masticated food, she struggled to get away.

The young man seated behind Kyle, who had observed them, jumped to her rescue, peeling Kyle off Caroline. Kyle elbowed the man in the gut, who then turned Kyle around and threw a punch, striking Kyle in the jaw. He went down to his knees.

Caroline could hear different patrons calling the police. Afraid of having her name and the connection with her father spelled out in the morning newspaper, she decided to split. Ducking her head, she was out the door as fast as her feet would carry her. Her Mustang was half a block away. Racing as fast as she dared, she fled the scene as two police cruisers screeched up the road with lights and sirens blaring.

CHAPTER NINETEEN

Caroline contacted the real estate agent Michael recommended. It was the same agent who had sold her the townhouse in the first place. "Thank you for taking this on."

The woman tsked. "It's no problem. I'm sorry you are moving out of Montpelier."

"Well, you know. The grass is always greener on the other side of the street. Besides, I lived in Fulton River with my parents for a time."

"True. This should be an easy process since I know the property so well. In fact, I might know someone who will snap it up immediately. If you didn't make many structural changes, I'll use the previous owner's photos. You don't mind. Do you?"

Caroline really wanted to showcase her home but knew it would be easier to use previous photos. "No. I didn't make any structural changes. Go ahead with the old photos."

"I expect this listing will go fast. So you should consider starting to pack."

True to her word, the agent listed the townhouse within twenty-four hours. Six hours after it was listed, Caroline had a decent offer. Having verified the minimum amount left on the mortgage with the agent, she accepted the cash offer even though it had one sticky point. Caroline had only two days to pack and move out.

She called Michael for help. "I have a deal on the townhouse. I need to move ninety percent of my things into storage. Can I get some money for that?"

"I didn't budget for it and I can't free up any more money. Perhaps your brother can fund the expense?" His reply left Caroline with no other choice but to contact Tony for money.

"Sure, Caro. I can loan you enough to get the storage units for a few months."

"Thanks," she said in a weary voice. "I'm not sure when I'll be able to pay you back for that money either."

"Don't worry. I trust you'll make good on the debt as soon as you can."

Caroline thought afterward that going into debt with her brother was a lot more hair-raising than using a credit card. There was familial trust there that she didn't want to disappoint. For the third time in her young life, she was grateful for her brother's help.

Tony's condo was not far from downtown Fulton River, off School Street. The complex sat on the bluff overlooking the Connecticut River, a not-so-wide expanse of water that separated Vermont from New Hampshire. Despite the location, Tony's condo unit was rather plain. The two-bedroom dwelling had a wide open space encompassing the living room, dining room, and kitchen areas. A large cathedral ceiling over the living room held a skylight, giving the area lots of sunlight during the daylight hours.

Caroline planted a kiss on his cheek. "Thank you for coming to my rescue yet again."

Tony hugged her tightly. "I'm glad I could help."

"I'm glad you never got rid of your condo." Caroline hugged him back and kissed his other cheek. "I can't believe mine sold so fast." It had been a whirlwind since she accepted the offer. The closing was tomorrow morning. Which necessitated vacating the premises as quickly as possible. Far quicker than she had ever anticipated despite the agent's warning. Tony had organized a moving crew that helped pack Caroline's things and transferred nearly everything to the local storage facility.

The two siblings stood in front of the condo's door. The day had been spent directing the movers on where everything should go. In the end, Tony had to pay for two large storage units for Caroline's extra furniture and belongings. Caroline wondered where all the stuff had come from. It was far more than she would have guessed.

QUEST FOR LOVE

The thought made her uneasy. Beyond the kitchen things she had moved to Tony's condo kitchen, Caroline could not think what the other twenty-seven boxes now in storage actually held. Tony had no clue, but he gave her his advice. "I will say this ... if you don't miss it in a couple of months, ask yourself if you really need it."

"I take your point," she replied. Truthfully, she remembered bringing home souvenirs from her travels with her friends. Did everything add up to so much? It didn't seem possible, but she doubted the packers had been under packing boxes. Instead, anything fragile would likely be found broken when she unpacked them.

"I promise I'll pay you back as soon as I get the money." She let go of her brother so he could leave. "Now, I'll be fine. I think I'll unpack some of my clothes."

"Good. Make yourself comfortable and keep me informed of your plans." He held out the condo key. "When you're finished using it, I'll have to put it back on the rental market."

She nodded. "I will let you know as soon as I know."

With a last nod, he left her alone in her temporary home.

Caroline shut the door and leaned back against it. The sight made her heart sink alongside her stomach. Tony's condo was tiny in comparison to her own. The four-room unit would suffice until the trust fund money came through. *Too bad the offering price wouldn't provide her with more income.* She had owned it for only six months before this fiasco happened, so there was no equity. Every cent of the sale would go toward paying off the mortgage. As Michael had said earlier when she texted him the news, "At least it's not a short sell." She had never heard the term before, but once she knew it meant selling below the remaining mortgage total, she too was grateful to be walking away free and clear.

As if on cue, Michael called. "I, um, wanted to appraise you of a new development." He paused, the tension in his voice clear through the silence.

"What is it?" Her body tensed, and her voice quivered. Whatever had happened, it wasn't good. "Tell me. Are they backing out of the deal?"

"The amount you accepted for the townhouse sale covers your mortgage. But it doesn't cover the outstanding property taxes."

Caroline closed her eyes and gripped the nearest stack of boxes as dizziness swirled in her head. "What property taxes?"

"The ones that should have been paid months ago." His tone was curt. "With the added late penalties, you're looking at more than five thousand dollars."

She exhaled heavily and closed her eyes. "Can I re-negotiate the sale terms?"

"Nope."

The silent air between them was heavy. "Are you sure your father didn't pay them?"

Michael's voice was firm and crystal clear. "I'm sure. It seems the terms of your original mortgage allowed the taxes to be taken out of escrow. But about four months ago, you had it changed to self-pay. But you never notified us. We can't pay bills we don't know anything about."

Caroline vaguely remembered having the mortgage company put the extra money toward the principle. She had meant to call Henry about paying the taxes. Now, she couldn't remember having done so.

She paced to the living room window and looked out at the green in the center of the complex. "What does that leave me with?"

"Less than two thousand dollars left for the next two weeks." After another brief pause, he asked, "How's the husband hunting going?"

"Fine." She knew her voice was too curt to make that statement believable. "I'm going on another date soon."

Michael's reply was just as curt. "Fine. Keep me posted." And the line went dead.

QUEST FOR LOVE

Caroline slumped against the wall beside an unstable stack of boxes. *Why, why, why is this nightmare happening to me?* The back of her head banged on the wall a half dozen times. She wasn't a bad person. Self-absorbed, maybe, but not bad. And she did a lot of things for other people. They appreciated her gifts of travel and cars, jewelry, and money. So what if she did it to keep her friends around her? It was the only protection she had. They kept her feeling safe and loved.

Since her wedding to David had been canceled, she had lived it up. Keeping busy organizing activities, travel, and such for her growing group of friends. Her plan had worked beautifully. She was always surrounded by a mixture of women and men. And never alone with a man. She made sure no man would get any ideas about sexual intimacy between them. Months of therapy had diminished the frequency of her nightmares but not her revulsion of a man's touch. Tony was the only male she allowed to hug her, kiss her cheek, or hold her hand. Randy had mesmerized her with his eyes and his words, won her trust and then became controlling and abusive. Between him and her childhood abuser, she would always think of sexual intimacy as something full of pain and dominance rather than an enjoyable experience. She wouldn't let it happen again.

There was nothing she could do about the townhouse sale situation except get back on her computer and search for another date. She had to find a husband. Time was running out.

CHAPTER TWENTY

"I uploaded my own profile on the dating app," Rachel announced.

Caroline thought she sounded smug. "Any luck yet?"

"Uh-huh. I've had several hits. There's one here from a guy named Patrick. He sounds nice, but his haircut in the picture looks like a crew cut. I'm not sure if I should answer."

Caroline signed on to her profile to check if anyone new had responded. "Okay, so maybe he's in the military, or—oh, I don't know. Why not inquire? Is he handsome?"

"Yeah, he is." Rachel sighed.

"What's his profile name? I'll look him up," Caroline offered, browsing the profiles of the men who had sent her messages. Some had texted her before, but she hadn't answered them. But there were a few new ones, including one called Staff of Chief. She hated it when there wasn't a photo. Especially when the profile name was something odd rather than a real name.

"Patty O."

Caroline searched and found the profile. "Oh, he is handsome. Too bad about the haircut. He'd look dynamite with a regular cut." She skimmed the profile contents and said, "He sounds rather bland."

Rachel replied, "Cute nickname, though."

"Maybe you should text him back. Find out more, like what he does for a living," Caroline said, clicking back to her own profile.

"Did you get anyone new?" Rachel asked.

Caroline scrolled down the list of profile IDs. "There's one here that sounds kind of risqué. Staff of Chief. The photo box was left blank and marked incognito." The website offered a service allowing members to pass a photo test within the company, and if their appearance and credentials checked out, their photo would be marked incognito. The purpose was to help members recognizable to the public protect their reputations for business or other reasons. . Caroline had considered using the service, but the extra two hundred dollar fee was over her budget. Michael hadn't balked at the $8.99 monthly fee, but she knew he'd nix the incognito fee.

"Hmm, interesting. Do you think he has an oversized staff he's trying to entice you with?"

Uncontrollable giggles erupted from Caroline. Leave it to Rachel to think in that twisted way. "I don't know, but I will reply to find out. He could be some creep trying to lure me with false promises of a long dick."

"Or he could be hung to his kneecaps." Rachel laughed, "Oops, an incoming call. Let me know, girlfriend."

The bio for the Staff sounded very corporate. *Perhaps he has a high-profile and high-salaried job.* Curious now, she responded to his message:

> Hi, thanks for contacting me. You sound very interesting.

She hit send and went back to perusing the list of messages. But in seconds, Staff replied in the chat feature:

> Why, thank you. I'm happy you are interested.

Caroline stared at his reply. He made it sound like she knew him or that they had met before. She wrote in the chat box:

> Do I know you?

His reply came in seconds later:

> Yes, we're acquainted. I've always hoped we could get to know each other better.

She blinked several times, her mind racing through her memory to figure out who he might be. She hoped it wasn't Kyle, Victor, or Daryl masquerading for revenge:

> Can you give me a clue where we've met before? A location or date or something?

She chewed her fingernail as she waited for his answer. The fact she had met him before was intriguing. Yet the butterflies in her stomach were not doing a happy dance. A niggling thought in the back of her mind was flashing a bright neon CAUTION sign.

> I really shouldn't tell you.

Unable to stop herself, she replied,

> Please tell me.

The cursor flickered in the text box where his response would show. One minute, two minutes. She was ready to give up on this teasing when the three dots appeared, indicating he was typing. The dots stopped. Then, ten seconds later, they started again. Her butterflies coalesced in the pit of her stomach. She was about to end the chat when his reply finally came.

> I'm acquainted with your father. I'd really like to take you out to dinner
> at Chez d'Avignon in Montpelier. It's a great place. Your parents and
> I have dined there numerous times.

QUEST FOR LOVE

He was a friend of her parents? How old was this guy? She checked his profile again. It was blank. Curious now, she asked:

> I'm twenty-two. How old are you?

The three dots disappeared for thirty seconds before bouncing. When they stopped, a message appeared:

> I'm less than twice your age but older than you.

She sat back in her chair and considered the reply and the invitation. The French restaurant was very high-class. The overpriced white-linen-tablecloth place was popular enough to be safe any day of the week. If necessary, she could flee just as she had with Kyle. Hopefully, a fist fight wouldn't break out this time.

His age was a little troublesome. Why hadn't he given her his age instead of being so cagy with it? Someone who knew her parents would likely treat her better than the past three dates. And if not, she knew how to leave. A great dinner at Chez d'Avignon would be awesome. Far better than the grilled peanut butter sandwiches or bowls of cereal that had been her dinners. She would have all her favorite dishes at the posh place: bouillabaisse, foie gras en croute, duck in muscat wine, and a chocolate soufflé for dessert. And she would eat every bite of it instead of being hypercritical about the calories.

Her stomach grumbled as the unease in her belly was replaced with hunger pains. Before she could change her mind, she typed:

> Fine. When shall I meet you there?

He swiftly replied:

> Wednesday night, at eight o'clock.

CHAPTER TWENTY-ONE

Taking Regina's instructions to heart, Caroline showed up on time and in sensible clothing for her first day at Jam Bakery. When she arrived at ten o'clock, the bakery traffic was slow. Most morning customers arrived before eight.

Jamaica gave her a tour of the bakery and the kitchen space hidden behind the swinging door. A tall blonde woman was transferring large plastic bins from a rolling cart to a long stainless steel table. Her green and white checkered apron covered the entire front of her clothing from her neck to her knees. Jamaica brought Caroline over to the table.

"Caroline, this is Isabelle Becker. Isabelle, this is Caroline Perret," Jamaica said.

As the two women shook hands, Jamaica added, "Isabelle manages the Jam Bakery shop in Windham, Vermont."

Caroline smiled. "I've heard it's the mecca for German baked goods."

"We set it up to sell all the same items available here, plus a lot of authentic German breads, cakes, cookies, and tarts," Isabelle explained. Her long blonde hair was pulled back and her lightly freckled cheekbones glowed with health. Caroline thought the woman's lack of makeup was scandalous. But the freshness of her appearance and her ready smile more than made up for the natural look.

"She's being very humble. Isabelle brought in all the recipes and helped develop them for commercial use," Jamaica interrupted. "And she speaks German. The customers of German ancestry love her."

Bright red splotches instantly formed over Isabelle's cheeks. "You're here to help me make jams?"

Caroline nodded. "I am. But I've never made anything before. Nothing as complicated as jam."

"You'll see, jam isn't complicated."

QUEST FOR LOVE

Jamaica interjected, "Ladies, I'm going to leave you to it." As the two women said their goodbyes, Jamaica headed for the dining room, disappearing with a swish of the swinging door.

"I can't believe Jamaica asked me to help." Caroline took the apron Isabelle handed her and put it on over her street clothes. "I don't know how much help I'll be, but I'll try."

Isabelle transferred the last of the items from the cart onto the table. "Our first step is to assemble all the ingredients and review the directions. I already gathered the things we'll need." She held up a piece of paper. "Here's the procedure."

Caroline glanced over the large bins of fruit: strawberries, raspberries, and cherries.

"Let's start with the strawberries. They've been washed already, so I'd like you to de-stem them and cut them into slices in this bowl." Isabelle plopped a large cooking pot before Caroline and placed a small knife beside it.

She stared at the heaping bin of strawberries. "Where do I start?"

A queer look flashed over Isabelle's face before disappearing into a tentative smile. "First, wash your hands. Then I'll show you."

Caroline glanced around the kitchen, noticed a large steel three-basin sink in the far corner, and headed for it.

"Not that one. That's for cleaning pots and pans," Isabelle called out before pointing to a small sink near the locker room doors. "Use that one."

She did as she was directed before returning to Isabelle's side. "Sorry." Isabelle gave her an apologetic smile. "I should have realized you've never worked in a commercial kitchen before. There are separate sinks for everything." She gestured to the small sink Caroline had just used. "That's for washing hands. As is that one." She gestured to a sink beside the sandwich prep area. "Those two," She pointed two fingers at medium-sized sinks near more stainless steel tables. "The left one is for washing fruits and vegetables. The right one is for meats." Then she pointed to the large sink Caroline had been walking toward initially. "Dishwashing. The left basin is for soapy water, the middle basin is rinse water, and the right basin is bleach water to sanitize the items."

Caroline stared at the different sinks. "Wow. Are all kitchens like this?"

"Yup. We need to keep the food safe from any potential contamination. The last thing we want to do is make our customers sick."

Nodding her understanding, Caroline stared down at the bin of strawberries again.

"You cut the stem and little green leaves off the top of the strawberry, then slice it into quarter-inch pieces, like so." Isabelle grabbed a strawberry and cut the top off, letting it fall into a waste basket between the two women. "Then you cut it into slices like so." The slices dropped into the cooking pot.

Caroline nodded. She didn't know what to say. It looked simple enough. "Do I slice up the entire bin?"

"Yes. We'll need all of them for our big batch of strawberry jam. Almost forty jars in one go." She handed over the paring knife. "I have to go wash the raspberries. I'll be right over there if you need me."

Again, Caroline nodded. Grasping the knife, she picked a berry out of the bin. She tried to cut the stem and leaves off in one swipe, but a few leaves stayed stuck to the berry. Caroline tried again. The leaves came off and the berry exuded bright red juice all over her hands. She set it down to wipe her hands on the dishtowel. With two fingers, she gingerly picked the berry up again and tried to slice it into the pot. Instead, the slices bounced off the rim onto the tabletop.

She didn't know what to do. *Should I place them in the pot, or is that a no-no?* Her gut felt a little odd as she stood there trying to decide whether she should ask Isabelle. Stiff with indecision, she waited for Isabelle to return with the freshly washed fruit.

QUEST FOR LOVE

"The slices hit the table instead of the pot. Are they usable, or should I trash them?"

Isabelle appeared at Caroline's side. "You can put those into the pot. I washed and disinfected the table before we started."

Caroline swiped them into her palm and dropped them into the pot. "That's one down."

Stunned, Isabelle whipped her head around. As she watched, Caroline gingerly picked up the next berry and treated it as if it had thorns, taking a full minute to individually cut all the leaves off the stem end, wipe her hands, and then slice the berry in half into the pot.

As Caroline reached for her third berry, Isabelle watched the second hand on the oversized clock near the swinging door. It was three minutes before the slices made a kerplunk sound in the pot. She closed her eyes briefly. At that rate, the bin would take Caroline all day to prep. She grabbed another knife from the table's drawer and a large bowl. "Let me help."

Thirty minutes later, the bin was empty. Caroline's pot held only fourteen cut berries. Isabelle's bowl held all the rest.

"I guess I'm pretty slow," Caroline said, an apologetic look on her face.

"You'll get the hang of it." Isabelle cringed at the lie. There was no way Caroline could keep up in this bakery. Isabelle would have to talk with Jamaica. But first, she had to get through this day. *Maybe we should have started with the raspberries. They only needed to be crushed.*

She handed Caroline a potato masher. "Now you have to crush the fruit slices."

Caroline gave the berries a mash. "Like that?"

"Good. Keep going. I'll be right back." Isabelle went off to find Jamaica. She considered herself a patient person, but she had never met anyone who moved so slowly. This wasn't going to work. There were four batches of fruit to jam before the bakery closed at four o'clock.

Ten minutes later, Isabelle lingered out of sight as Jamaica entered the kitchen. "Caroline. Don't forget to take a half-hour lunch break. Go order yourself some lunch. It's on the house."

Caroline wiped her hands on the dishtowel. "Okay. All this fruit smells so good it's making me hungry." She did as she was told, disappearing through the swinging door.

Only then did Isabelle join Jamaica at the table to survey how little work got done in the last hour.

When Caroline returned, Isabelle was ladling hot strawberry jam into jars. "What can I do?"

Isabelle's hand continued filling and capping the jars as she spoke. "I'm ready to put these in the hot water bath. Why don't you start on the raspberries? Take the potato masher and crush the pot full of raspberries."

She did as instructed, getting the masher and crushing all the berries. *This is easier than strawberries.* When she was finished, Isabelle called to her. "How's it going?"

Caroline spun around to answer, but her hand holding the masher in the pot moved with her. It only took a nanosecond for the entire pot of bright red crushed raspberries to tip and spill all over her shoes on the way to the floor. Shocked by the cold puree, she could only stand there, her throat unable to form any words. At last, she whispered, "I'm sorry." She covered her face with her hands. The pot tumbled to the floor with a clang as it bounced a few times and rolled away.

Isabelle rushed over, trying to stand clear of the spreading pool of fruit. "Are you okay?"

Suddenly, Jamaica was there. Seeing the disaster, she put her arm around Caroline's shoulders. "Take off your shoes. We'll get you cleaned up in a jiffy. But I don't think you'll be wearing those shoes ever again."

Caroline stared down at her former black Gucci loafers, now covered in crushed raspberries and their juices. "I don't think so either." She looked up into Jamaica's eyes. "I don't think I'm cut out for baking work. I'm sorry."

Jamaica hugged her sideways, her arm still wrapped around Caroline's shoulders. "That's all right. Not everybody gets the hang of it. I'll think of something. Come back on Thursday at about nine o'clock."

Caroline went back to Tony's condo feeling like a dog with its tail between its legs. At least she had plenty of time to clean up, take a nap, and get ready for her date that evening.

CHAPTER TWENTY-TWO

It was dusk when Caroline opened the elaborately carved double doors to Chez d'Avignon. She approached the vacant maître d's station, looking around to observe the diners seated at identical white flaxen linen cloth-covered tables. Despite the late hour and the mid-week night, the place bustled with staff and customers.

I wonder if someone I know is here. The last thing she wanted was someone to see her with her date and run to her mother or father with the news. She was glad she had spent more time on her toilette. The confidence the stunning red Hermès dress gave her added to the excitement of meeting this mystery man and the sensational meal to come. Her red, patent leather four-inch heeled pumps clicked on the marble tiled floor as she paced the station.

The maître d hurried to her side. "Ma cher mademoiselle Perret! It has been too long since you graced us with your presence." He took both her hands in his and kissed her on each cheek. "Just this past Saturday, your papa and mamma dined here with friends."

Caroline felt the earth shift beneath her feet, knowing her parents had been here for dinner over the past weekend. She thanked God neither of them had shown up tonight.

His eyes sparkled mischievously. "I understand you are meeting someone here this evening."

"Oui, Monsieur Lavau. I am meeting someone special tonight." It was true. She and Staff of Chief had texted since their first exchange earlier in the week. She found his comments and questions intriguing and his sense of humor entertaining. Finally being here, soon to meet him, had her stomach in a flutter. Caroline had a very good feeling about this man from the conversations that passed between them in the last few days. Perhaps he would be the answer to her prayers.

"This way, Mademoiselle." He picked up two menus and led her to a quiet table in the back of the dining room.

QUEST FOR LOVE

The elaborately set table sparkled with Baccarat crystal water and wine goblets. The cream-colored Limoges porcelain plates sat on gold-toned chargers. An open champagne bottle chilled in its bucket beside the table.

Her shoulders fell at the sight of the two empty chairs. "Is monsieur not here yet?" She turned to the maître d'.

"Oui, but he stepped into the adjoining banquet room to greet the mayor." Seeing her anxious look, he added, "I will inform him of your arrival." He pulled out her chair and chivalrously settled her into it.

Monsieur Lavau handed her a menu and placed one on her date's charger before hustling off to find him.

With nothing else to do, Caroline reviewed the menu. It had a few new additions, but all her favorites were still offered. Her stomach growled as her mouth watered at the impending gastronomic delights the night held in store. And if she were equally lucky, this fourth date might be her last.

Monsieur Lavau returned. "Monsieur says he will be right with you, ma cher. May I get you anything to drink while you wait?"

She eyed the champagne but decided it would be impolite to indulge before her date arrived. "No, merci. I'll wait."

He bowed slightly. "Oui, Mademoiselle. Très bien." He turned and strode away.

With nothing else to do but wait, she eyed the tables surrounding her. The aromas enticed her stomach to growl again. She hadn't had much food at lunch today, so she could indulge on tonight's dinner. Until she got her hands on that trust money, this would be the only time she could eat here. At over three hundred dollars per person per night, not including alcohol, it was far beyond her budget.

She jumped in her seat as fingertips brushed her shoulder. She turned to smile up at her date, but the smile vanished instantly. She gasped, then covered her mouth as her heart raced uncontrollably and her body recoiled from his touch.

"Have I surprised you, my dear?" Donald Sarlin leered as he pulled out his chair and sat down.

Caroline jumped up from the table so fast her chair flipped over backward. Her hands wringing, she stared into eyes that haunted her dreams. Her throat thick, she couldn't say anything. She turned to run, bumped into the champagne stand, and spilled ice water all over the floor. With a thud, the bucket landed, spewing a gush of champagne as it rolled away.

Donald flew to her side, but Caroline stumbled backward into the next table, knocking it over to the aghast cries of the diners. The crash of crystal and splintering porcelain drew more attention to her reaction.

"S-Stay away from me." Her eyes not leaving her predator's, shards of crystal crunched under her shoes as she backed farther away.

He stepped after her, his hand outstretched. "Come, my dear. We should talk."

As she continued to shrink back, he lunged forward, gripping her wrist.

Caroline screamed, "Get your hand off me! Let me go!" She twisted, freeing her hand from his grasp as the maître d' stepped between them.

"Mademoiselle, are you all right?"

Again, her eyes did not leave Donald's. "I need to leave, Monsieur Lavau. Please escort me to my car."

Mr. Lavau did not hesitate. "Bien sur." He lightly pressed his hand to the small of her back and led her out to the front of the restaurant.

She slipped behind the wheel of her car as Monsieur Lavau asked, "Are you all right?"

She nodded, trying not to let the tears springing to her eyes show.

Caroline held it together throughout the long ride back to Fulton River. Once inside Tony's condo, she locked the door and checked it twice. Slumping against the wall and sliding down to the floor, she wrapped her arms around her knees and rocked, crying as she hadn't cried in years. Not since that day, thirteen years ago, when Donald Sarlin, her father's senatorial chief of staff, attacked her on the sofa in her father's library. The day he silenced her screams with his crushing mouth while his fingers groped up her dress until they hurt her.

With shaking hands, she deleted the app from her phone and vowed never to search online dating sites ever again.

The phone ringing woke Caroline. She glanced at her cell phone. It was a quarter to midnight.

"Where *are* you?" Rachel demanded.

Caroline rubbed her eyes. "I'm home."

"No, you're not. Want to know how I know that?" Sarcasm dripped with every word she spoke.

Caroline felt her heart skip a beat. She hadn't told anyone she sold her townhouse and moved into Tony's Fulton River condo. "Let me guess, I didn't answer the doorbell."

"No! You didn't! Some strange man did and told me *he* owns the place now. I'm lucky he didn't greet me with a firearm or send the cops after me. You sold it?" She sounded hurt. Rachel seemed more upset that Caroline hadn't told her about the sale rather than that she had rang a stranger's doorbell at midnight.

"It—" Caroline started, trying to figure out on the fly how to explain the sudden sale and her neglecting to mention it. "It was a sudden decision. I moved into Tony's condo." The heavy breathing in her ear made her continue. "It's temporary."

"Temporary?" Rachel huffed. "Girlfriend, selling your home is not 'temporary.' What is going on with you? First, you back out of the Gala and cancel our trip to France, then you're looking for a husband, and now you've sold your home!" A heavy sigh filled Caroline's ear. "What is happening? Are you possessed?"

Caroline pressed her palm to her forehead, thinking hard about whether she wanted to tell Rachel the truth. "I—I'm a little low on funds. So, I sold my townhouse. Tony's letting me stay in his place for a few months until the situation can get straightened out."

Rachel huffed. "Low on funds? Are you kidding me? You got three million just a year ago."

"I know. I know. Believe me, I know. But I kinda went overboard with the spending. Besides, the townhouse was too big. And I think I might make Fulton River my home instead of Montpelier."

When Rachel didn't respond, Caroline added, "Okay—so that's it. Now, why did you try to contact me? What's going on with you?" She wanted to change the subject as quickly as possible so Rachel wouldn't ask any more questions.

"I just had the most amazing date. He was so rizz!" She gushed. "And I wanted to tell you about it."

"I'm glad someone did," Caroline muttered.

Rachel continued, "I think I've found the one, except he's really not my type."

Caroline sat up in bed and turned on the bedside table lamp. Mistake. Her swollen, light-sensitive eyes could not tolerate the brightness, so she turned the lamp off again. "Rach, you're not making sense. How can he be the one if he's not your type?"

"We met at this little place called The Vanilla Bean. It was like a hippy-era coffeehouse, complete with a stage. We had some great burgers while we talked. And then, this folk singer comes on stage and sang these heartfelt songs, and we held hands ..."

"You and the singer held hands?" Her brain was feeling foggy, incapable of catching Rachel's words as she sped through them like a fish darting through a river.

Rachel giggled. "No, silly. Patrick and I held hands. It was so rad." The tone of her voice changed to stern. "And listen up—he's a cop. I can't date a cop."

"Oh." Caroline didn't know what to say. On the one hand, it was weird he was a working man, and yet, Rachel seemed smitten with him.

QUEST FOR LOVE

He was very different from the men in their social circle. All of them were rich enough to not have to work. Or at least held positions in family businesses that paid them a salary for no real work at all. *Like David had done.*

A hint of tension filled Rachel's voice. "What do you mean, 'oh'?"

She closed her eyes and slumped back on the pillows. "Can we talk about this tomorrow? I'm not feeling so well."

"What's going on?" Suspicion filled her voice. "OMG! You had another date tonight, didn't you? Is he there?"

Caroline's voice became a whisper as tears filled her eyes again. "It was him. And he touched me." Just thinking about it made her want to take another long, hot shower. But her skin couldn't take a third scrubbing in less than four hours.

Silence, then a quick intake of breath as Rachel figured out who she was referring to. Then she blurted, "Ohmygod. Him as in *him*? Are you okay? Do you want to talk? Should I come over?"

Caroline could use her friend's company. And she might feel a little more secure if someone were with her. She prayed Donald didn't know where she was staying. He might have found her address online and paid a visit. *If he had gone there to find me, if I hadn't moved away...* She placed her palm over her eyes. That was not a scenario she wanted to think about. "I'm okay. I don't think he knows where I'm staying."

"Do you want to talk about it?"

Caroline paused as she debated the offer. "Not tonight. I just want to go back to sleep. I took a couple of sleeping pills. I don't think I'll sleep otherwise."

"You call me if you change your mind. I don't want you to be alone."

A chill raced down her spine. That pervert was out there somewhere. "Can we meet up tomorrow afternoon at Jam Bakery? I'm working my second day there."

"You're *working*? Good God, girlfriend, you've got lots of explaining to do."

They made arrangements to meet soon and disconnected the call.

Caroline flicked back the bed linens and padded to the condo door. *Just once more. I'll check the locks just once more.* She triple-checked the normal doorknob lock and the deadbolt. Both were secure. Standing on her tiptoes, she looked out the peephole. The outside porch light was still on. No one was in sight.

She leaned back against the wall beside the door. The feeling of dread was lifting in increments. The living room was bathed in moonlight. Between that and the smallness of the room, she felt like she was in a cave. Surrounded by indestructible walls with only one way in or out. Walking to the couch, she picked up the throw, cocooned herself in it, and sat facing the door. She would not be surprised again.

CHAPTER TWENTY-THREE

Jam Bakery was still busy with the morning crowd when Caroline arrived just before nine o'clock on Thursday morning. Over the last three hours, she had contemplated canceling this lesson. Taking a deep breath of the fresh bread-scented air, her stomach growled. If she could have a steaming slice this minute, she'd slather it with butter and sink her teeth into it.

Walking through the kitchen, she saw a baby-faced man pulling round loaves of bread out of an oven with a large paddle. He worked quickly, transferring them from the heat to the cooling racks set on the stainless steel table beside the oven. He noticed her, stopped what he was doing, and held up his index finger as if asking her to wait.

She halted in her tracks and waited while he took the last two steaming hot loaves out of the oven. After closing the oven door and setting down the paddle, he approached.

"I'm Mark. In charge of bread baking." He wiped his hands on the towel he pulled from his apron belt. A light cloud of flour emanated from the cloth when he shook it out and tucked it on the apron string. "You must be Caroline."

She smiled halfheartedly and nodded. "That's me. Back for another go at working here."

"Isabelle isn't here today." His grin quirked into a comedic smile. "You'll be working with my girlfriend, Jackie Thorndike. You're in luck.
"

"What makes you say that? Is she better at making jam than Isabelle?"

"Not necessarily. But she's a natural-born teacher. She's an instructor at King Mills Flour Company. If anyone can teach you something about making jam, Jackie's your girl."

Caroline tilted her head to the side. "I vaguely remember hearing about her. She used to be head bread baker here, wasn't she?"

The man nodded, a lock of hair flopping down on his forehead with the movement. "Yup, that's my girl." A smile stretched across his face as he looked over Caroline's shoulder. "Here she comes."

Caroline turned around to see a short, voluptuous woman approaching from Jamaica's office. She extended her hand before she was ten feet away.

"Caroline. It's a pleasure to work with you today."

"Same here. Thank you. I appreciate the second opportunity."

Jackie threaded her arm around Caroline's elbow. "Well, you're a beginner. We have to start from the beginning, not throw you into the mixing pot and expect you to swim."

Mark shook his head. "What a mixed-up metaphor that is! I'll leave you to your project."

Over the next half hour, Jackie explained and showed Caroline all the equipment spread out on the stainless steel table. The scale for weighing amounts, the liquid measures, the different hand mixing tools, and their uses. Caroline thought it was brilliant to learn what something was and how to use it properly. Something Isabelle had not realized was lacking in Caroline's education. At least not until it was too late.

Then Jackie described the chemical process that turned crushed fruit into jam. Some of the words were familiar to Caroline. As a young child, she was a frequent visitor to her parents' kitchen, where the full-time cook made everything from scratch. The cook would tell Caroline what she was doing at each step to keep the child entertained. If Caroline helped by fetching things or stirring pots, she was rewarded with a spatula or spoon covered with sweet batters, frosting, or jam residue to lick as a treat.

It wasn't until nearly ten o'clock that they started making jam.

"Today, we're going to start with raspberries." Jackie gestured to the pot full of glossy, bright red berries.

QUEST FOR LOVE

Flutters erupted in Caroline's gut. *I hope they don't end up on the floor or ruin my clothes and shoes again.* She admired the luscious-looking fruit. "They're beautiful. Where did they come from?"

Jackie picked two out of the pot and dropped one into Caroline's hand, then popped the second into her mouth. "They come from Dutton's in Newfane. They have terrific berries."

Very slowly, Jackie talked Caroline through the process one step at a time. Caroline was astounded she was actually doing the work while Jackie directed her movements. Not only did she tell her what to do, but she also told Caroline what to watch for: color changes, viscosity changes, crystallization, and bubbling in the pot.

Within another half hour, they were filling sterilized glass jars with the finished jam slurry. Together, they sealed the jars and placed them in the hot water bath to further sterilize and vacuum seal them.

They stepped out for a break after the jars were processed.

"I can't believe how easy it is," Caroline said. "Once I understood everything, it's quite fun." Indeed, not long after Jackie had started going over the equipment, all of Caroline's jitters evaporated.

"It's easy if you prepare everything and measure everything ahead of time. That way, you are less likely to get caught with your pants down at the wrong time."

"So when do we label the jars?" Caroline asked before taking a bite of her almond croissant.

Jackie nodded as she finished chewing hers. "We'll label them when the jars cool. Maybe tomorrow."

"Tomorrow?" Jamaica inquired as she approached the table. "How did it go today?"

"Terrific. I learned so much in the last two hours. It all makes sense now in my brain. I like making jam." Caroline decided she should give credit where credit was due. "Jackie is an awesome instructor." She turned toward Jackie. "Thank you for making this feeble woman into a jam maker. At least for today."

"Just today?" Jamaica asked, one eyebrow raised. "Lots more jam needs to get made while the berries are still fresh."

"I'd love to help. But I'm not sure about the next two weeks. I have a vacation rental near Acadia National Park."

Jamaica waved her hand. "Don't worry, we make jam off and on all through the summer as different fruits become ripe. Let me know when you get back. It'll be time for peaches."

As Caroline packed up her things to leave, she realized Rachel hadn't shown up. Is this payback for standing her up at their Sunday meeting times? Or was something up with her? She decided to let it slide.

CHAPTER TWENTY-FOUR

She strode into Michael's waiting room, ready for a fight with his receptionist. She didn't have an appointment but needed to talk to him. Both Jamaica and Regina had paid her with a paper check. She didn't have a clue what to do with it, but she knew Michael would have the answer. The receptionist's desk was empty. Not a single thing remained on it. Caroline peered over the desktop. Gabriella's chair was pushed under the desk as much as possible. *Maybe she's on vacation. But why were all her photos and her computer missing?* Michael's inner office door was ajar, and Caroline could hear an argument on the other side. It was the first time she had heard Michael's raised voice. Reluctant to intrude at such a heated moment, she quietly sat on the chair closest to the door and listened.

An unfamiliar voice shouted, "I did everything Pop told me to do. I dreamed big and studied hard. I got my ass accepted into Harvard. Now you're telling me I can't go?"

Michael replied, "I'm sorry. I can't afford Harvard University. Why not go to a community college for the first year? Take all your required general education courses there. That gives me more time to straighten out our finances. You can transfer into Harvard for your sophomore year."

"I don't want to go to some two-bit community college. I deserve to go to Harvard, damn it!" His last words were punctuated by a pounding sound. Probably his fist on Michael's desk, Caroline thought.

Silence.

"Look, Alan," Michael said. "I don't like this situation any better than you do. I'd *love* to send you off to Harvard. But I just can't afford it. This business is underwater. I haven't had a paycheck in weeks." His voice trembled as he spoke. "I had to let Gabriella go. I can't afford her salary any longer."

Had Caroline heard correctly? Was the accountant going bankrupt? Wasn't he supposed to be the financial expert? Her teeth clenched. Maybe she should find another accountant.

Caroline realized the other male was Michael's younger brother. Alan's voice was so soft she almost couldn't hear it. "How are we surviving then? You bring home money for groceries and utilities. I've seen you hand it to Mom." The accusation in his tone was unmistakable.

"I have a rainy day fund. A year's worth of savings for a bad situation like this. It's getting depleted rather swiftly." Michael's voice cracked. He sounded like a broken man. Caroline's heart gave a pang of sympathy. He was going through what she was going through. Except he had dependents. A mother, a sister, and two younger brothers. Alan must be the one graduating high school.

Alan spoke in a softer voice, "I had no idea. I thought we were doing well. Dad had a lot of wealthy clients, didn't he?"

"That he did. But he let them overspend. The best I can figure is that when their accounts were overdrawn, Dad filled the gap with the business's money."

"But why? That sounds like a stupid thing to do."

"I agree. He covered as much as he could. He considered it a no-interest loan and notified the clients. Some paid the business back. Others blew him off."

"Why didn't he say anything to them. Let them know they were overspending?"

"Come on, Alan. Dad never wanted to deal with people or problems like that. He wanted to bury his nose in his figures. Why do you think he never had anything to do with our upbringing? It wasn't because he was super busy at work. He didn't want to confront any one of us about anything, including Mom."

"Mom wasn't much better." Alan's voice was low and accusing.

"Neither of our parents were very good at parenting. It's a wonder we're turning out well."

"I'll say. But we always had you. You were there for us. Keeping us on the straight and narrow."

"Somebody had to."

"I can't get over the fact Dad spent all that money shoring up client's accounts but never insisted they pay him back."

"Maybe he did. Some did reimburse him. Others ... perhaps they were ashamed, maybe they didn't want to pay him back. I really don't know." Someone cleared their throat. It must have been Michael because his words scratched as he spoke, as though he had a lump in his throat. "What matters is, whatever savings this business had are gone. Gone because of Dad's kindness."

Caroline's heart ached. Was she one of the reasons? Had Henry paid her bills while she spent money unchecked? Had she been part of the problem?

"Aren't there any clients we can approach to pay the money back?" Alan must not have liked the look on his brother's face. "You haven't gone after them, have you." It was more a confirmatory statement than a question.

A heavy sigh. "It's not that easy. Some of these people are bankrupt. They don't have the ability to repay the business. Others have left Vermont for parts unknown. It takes a lot of effort to track them down. More than I can do while sustaining the current clients and their problems."

Her head slipped back to rest against the wall as tears came to her closed eyes. They spilled down her face. She was sure she was one of the clients he was referring to. As much as she wanted to save Michael and his family, she couldn't. Not now.

Michael's office door opened abruptly. She snapped to her feet, her eyes wide, startled by the sound.

"Caroline?" Michael spoke as though disbelieving it was her.

Her palm swiped her tear-stained face. "I—I'm sorry. I—" She stopped.

Alan, a thin, young man not much taller than Michael, looked her up and down with a disdainful expression. "Is this one of them?"

Michael didn't answer. His cringe either answered the question or meant he disapproved of Alan asking such a personal question. Caroline couldn't decide which.

Alan gave her a sneer before pounding out the office door.

Michael's eyes diverted elsewhere rather than look at her. "We didn't have an appointment, did we?"

She shook her head. Michael buried his face in his hands momentarily. The misery etching his features took her breath away. "I can come back another time."

He shook his head slowly. "No. Let's talk." He motioned her into his office.

CHAPTER TWENTY-FIVE

This time, Michael sat in the chair beside hers in front of his desk. *He really should get a sofa or loveseat for these less formal conversations with clients.* Their chairs were angled toward each other, their knees almost touching. For a fleeting second, Caroline wanted to press her kneecap to his. As though he read her mind, he stared at her before sitting up straighter. The space between their knees widened a couple more inches, and they both stared at the gulf between them.

"If you overheard my discussion with Alan, I need to explain." He placed his palms over his knees and leaned forward.

"What's my part in all this mess? Did your father pay anything for me?"

Michael met her eyes. "He did. And he also stopped taking his accounting fees out of your checking account."

Caroline pressed her lips together. It had been a long time since she had seen an invoice from Henry. She remembered Michael mentioning she owed the business thousands of dollars. "I want to pay it all back."

He frowned. "It's more than you can pay back at this time."

For the thousandth time in twenty-four hours, she resolved to marry. "I will pay you back every penny with interest once I get my hands on the rest of that trust money."

His head dropped, his chin resting on his chest. "I'm not sure I can wait that long."

Her heart squeezed with longing to fix the situation. She pulled the two checks from her purse. "Take these."

Michael's fingers brushed hers as he took the slips of paper. "What are these?"

"My first two paychecks." A surge of pride filled her chest. "There'll be more after I return from Mount Desert Island. If I don't find someone to marry by then."

She chided herself for not finding a husband in the last two weeks. Every date she had been on had been a disaster. Except the last one. That had been a true nightmare. A shiver ran through her body.

"Are you cold, Caroline? I have a sweater—"

She stood and began pacing the office. "No, thank you. I need to think."

Silently, Michael watched her as she traveled from one end of the room to the other. She needed a husband and fast. But someone who would marry her temporarily, then quietly divorce her, take his share of the money, and leave her alone. Sign a prenup to do it, too. A thought popped into her mind. She also needed someone who wouldn't want to consummate the marriage. No physical contact had to be agreed upon in the prenup. But what man would agree to do all that? Why couldn't she find a man who was handsome, agreeable, and with whom she could talk with, really talk with, like Michael DeBois?

"Can I help?" Michael interrupted her thoughts.

Can he help? The phrase sank into her brain like a tomahawk. Instead of blood, the solution to the problem erupted. Their mutual problem. She raised her eyes to heaven and stood beside him. "I have a brilliant idea." She stared into his eyes with an overwhelming feeling of wonder at the simplicity of the solution.

A wary glimmer shone in his eyes, but he remained silent. He waved his hand as though encouraging her to continue.

"The solution to my problem, as in finding a husband, and your problem, as in getting money to send Alan to Harvard and keep the business going ... they're the same."

His forehead crinkled. "I don't understand." He shifted his position in the chair as if he were suddenly uncomfortable.

"It's easy." Caroline dropped to one knee. "Michael, will you marry me?"

QUEST FOR LOVE

His mouth dropped open, but no sound emerged. Even his heart stilled in place.

"I know. It's pretty drastic, but I think it's the perfect solution. We get married, you get the money you need for Alan's education, and I pay you back the money I owe. After a couple months, we go our separate ways."

Blinking wildly, Michael finally said, "I don't think that's ethical."

Caroline's exasperated sigh filled the space between them. "Look. It's a business arrangement. I'm willing to give you a million dollars to marry me and divorce me. But there's one stipulation. No intimacy between us." She stared at him like she was willing him to say yes. "It'll all be spelled out in the prenup. The money, the intimacy prohibition. Even the length of the marriage if you want it. Just say yes."

His mind raced with the possibilities. One million would be a hefty sum. It would easily cover the $300,000 to send Alan to Harvard for four years. That would leave him with $700,000 to shore up the business, hire Gabriella back, set some aside for Jason's college education, and maybe even save a chunk for retirement. *So what are the cons?*

I can't sleep with her.

It dawned on him that if he married her, he would want intimacy. She was beautiful, graceful, and kind to her friends. Overly kind, especially to all those so-called friends who helped get her into this predicament.

"What will you tell your friends?"

Her eyes widened. "My friends? What friends? They've all but forgotten me now that I can't take them on trips or indulge their every whim. Besides, they don't need to know. We can keep it a secret. Who needs to know anyway besides the trust fund administrator?"

Caroline got up off her knee and sat in her chair. "It's a contract. But we should make it look like we're really married. I don't want the trust administrator to get suspicious." Her eyes widened, gleaming with excitement. "I just thought of something. We can go to the house I rented on Mount Desert Island. Just for a week or so. Like it's a honeymoon, except we'll have separate bedrooms."

The positive ramifications of agreeing to marry her were outstanding. But could he maintain a physical distance from her, even with a prenup contract? For a million dollars?

Michael looked Caroline in the eyes. "Yes, I'll marry you."

CHAPTER TWENTY-SIX

The two of them met with Michael's attorney the following day. Together, Caroline and Michael hashed out the terms of the contract with the attorney's help. Divorce after six months and no intimacy during the marriage. The attorney had remarked that it was an unusual term for a prenup. He talked them both into a clause stating Michael would not receive more than a million-dollar settlement if they divorced in less than four months. Feeling her usual generosity and despite Michael's protestations, Caroline had him add that Michael would receive an additional half million dollars if it lasted beyond a year.

Michael insisted on a week's stay on Mount Desert Island. Just the two of them. The purpose being, he had told her privately, they wanted to appear to be really in love, rather than it look like a fraud. He was worried the executor of the trust fund would raise red flags about the marriage and the subsequent money distribution if it ended too quickly.

After leaving the attorney's office, they went to the Fulton River Town Hall. In the clerk's office, Michael bought the marriage license.

As they left the building, he asked, "Where do you want to get married?" He opened the car door for Caroline before sliding into the passenger seat beside her in her Mustang.

She sat behind the wheel, clutching it with white-knuckled hands. "I hadn't given it much thought. We can get married anywhere in the state. What do you think?"

She gazed at him with her big doe eyes. He saw the hint of fear deep within them. *What is she so afraid of? She ought to know I'm not going to hurt her.* "Funny you should ask that. Driving through Haston last weekend, I saw a sign at an inn that said something like, Justice of the Peace 24/7."

"Really? Huh, sounds like the right place." She started the car. "Do you know how to get back there?"

With a nod, Michael directed her to the highway, and then they followed the signs for the town of Haston.

CHAPTER TWENTY-SEVEN

The stately white inn gave Caroline the impression of a southern plantation house with its wide veranda at ground level and a balcony veranda off the second story of the building. Dark green rocking chairs with woven reed seats and tall backrests adorned the lower veranda. The front of the first two stories was of a mottled white and maroon brick, while the third level was wrapped in white clapboards. The hanging shingle sign off the porch declared it The Tavern Inn.

The reception area was colonial in style, with a small wood fire burning in the fireplace. Windsor chairs and polished wood tables gave it a simple elegance.

The receptionist, Mrs. Paulson, beamed on seeing them. "How may I help you?" she asked. "Do you have a reservation?"

Michael stepped forward to manage the details. "We were wondering if the justice of the peace was still available."

Her smile widened even further. "Yes, my husband can perform a civil marriage if that is what you are looking for." She pulled out a brochure. "We can offer you a simple service for one hundred dollars, or we have a package that includes the service, one night at the inn, plus dinner and breakfast in our restaurant for three hundred." She looked from one to the other of them. "There's a third package that includes photography for five hundred dollars. Would you like me to see if the photographer is available?

"No need for formal pictures," Caroline said, placing a hand on Michael's arm.

Michael shot her a grimace. "Don't we want something to show to those who might not believe we were married?"

Caroline and Michael stared at each other silently.

Mrs. Paulson looked from one to the other with a perplexed look. "I can always take a few with your cell phones. No additional charge."

Michael spoke up, "We'll take the second package."

Caroline blurted out, "Do you have a room with two beds?"

The woman's smile faltered. "Two beds?" She glanced at her book. Her finger sweeping the page. "I'm afraid rooms with more than one bed are already occupied."

Caroline tensed. She had asked herself if they could share a room. Now, she'd have to share a bed. Could she trust Michael to stick to the contract? *If I can't trust him tonight, I can't trust him at all.* She chewed on her lower lip. She had made the stipulation, and Michael had agreed. He'd signed his name to the contract in the attorney's office. She would have to trust him, or it wasn't worth saying "I do." And if she wanted to get that money and get back to her normal life, she would have to go through with their plan. Her plan. "We'll take it."

The woman's smile brightened. "What time would you like the ceremony?"

"As soon as possible," Caroline replied.

Seeing the look on Caroline's face, a look she deciphered as impatience, Mrs. Paulson picked up the phone and dialed. "Honey, there's a couple here who want to get married." After a few seconds, she hung up. "He'll be down in thirty minutes. Why don't you two step into the living room and relax while you wait." She gestured through the arched doorway. "Unless you'd like to go to your room and freshen up or change into wedding attire."

Caroline glanced down at her light blue cashmere sweater and navy pencil skirt. In no way did it qualify as wedding attire. A glance at Michael proved he was no better off. His white, button down Oxford shirt might be the correct color, but his jeans and Nike trainers served him well as office casual, but they would never do for a wedding.

She chuckled to herself, thinking how very different this wedding was going to be compared to the elaborate hoopla her mother had wanted for her wedding with David. Mrs. Perrett would have a stroke if she were here to witness this event with no cake, no flowers, no photographer, no band, no tent, and no bridal party. Not to mention the lack of press releases about the engagement and nuptials to all the Vermont and Washington, D.C. newspapers.

Caroline turned to Michael and shook her head.

"No, thank you," Michael said in a rush of words. He couldn't help but think he was making a huge mistake. And if he went out to the car for the luggage, he might change his mind. Pressing a hand to the small of her back, he guided Caroline into the living room. Another small fire in what appeared to be an original stone hearth lit the room. He strode to one of the two wing-backed armchairs beside it. Caroline sat in the other chair. She leaned her head back against the cushion and closed her eyes. Was she feeling the same jitters? Was she also questioning the wisdom of doing this, of playing out the plan she had devised? It was hard to tell. Her face was serene. Perhaps she was meditating?

His phone chirped with a text message notification. It was Alan.

> Mom said you closed the office and you're going away for one week. What's going on?

He pondered his reply. What should he say? He decided to keep the facts hidden for now.

> I'm going to Mount Desert Island on vacation. I need a break. Time to think. I'll let you know when I'm home.

Alan's reply didn't take long.

> Dude, you never go on vacation. Besides, I have to send Harvard an answer. What should I tell them?

And there was the fortification he needed to get through the ceremony. He squared his shoulders and fired back a reply.

> Tell them yes you'll be going. Now leave me alone so I can figure out how to pay for it.

He turned off the phone and shoved it into his pants pocket just as an older man dressed in a navy blue three-piece suit entered the room. He carried what looked to be a small pocket-sized book. "Ready?"

Mr. Paulson, the justice of the peace, assembled them before the fireplace when his wife, the receptionist and witness arrived. Taking first Michael's right hand, and then Caroline's, the justice of the peace placed them together and began the ceremony by speaking with the usual, "Dearly beloved ..." Michael could feel her palm was cold and clammy. He willed his warmth toward her. Gradually, the heat between them built as their hands remained joined. Mr. Paulson spoke eloquently about marriage being a gift given to comfort the sorrows of life and to magnify life's joys.

Was marriage a comfort? It certainly hadn't been in his parents' life. By the time he was able to perceive the relationship between his parents, Michael had known their lives were separate. They did things separately and ate separately. They even slept separately. It wasn't until he was in high school that he realized spouses usually slept together.

Michael cringed at the impediment part. Wasn't fraud an impediment? Or, at the very least, coercion? But he remained silent, as did Caroline, and the JP went on without stopping for more than a glance between them.

The rest of the ritual went by in a blur. When asked, he managed to repeat, "I, Michael Henry DuBois, take you, Caroline Rose Perret, to be my wife. To have and to hold from this day forward, for better or for worse, for richer or for poorer, in sickness and in health. I promise to love, honor, cherish, and protect you all the days of my life until death do us part."

Mr. Paulson turned to Caroline and asked her to repeat the same vow. Bug-eyed, she stared at him, then at Michael. Seconds of silence passed while Caroline continued to stare, her eyes fearful.

Am I so repulsive that she really doesn't want to marry me? Is the jig up? He had always thought he'd be the one most likely to back out of the plan. Yet, there she stood, trembling, biting her lower lip and not uttering a sound.

"Miss Perret?" Mr. Paulson repeated. When she didn't respond, he turned to Michael. "Don't fret, it's just nerves."

Michael knew it wasn't just nerves. It was the whole situation. She had no choice if she wanted to return to her over-the-top life of ease and parties, travel, and luxury. "Caroline?" he whispered, squeezing her hands gently.

Caroline's mind raced with the images and feelings of that one afternoon in her father's library. Sitting pretty and polite on the sofa beside her father's chief of staff. His personal questions, his leering eyes, his unnerving predatory smile. He'd pounced, grabbing the back of her neck and pulling her closer. Slamming his mouth down on hers. She had struggled as his free hand snaked up her skirt and peeled down her underwear with a yank. Thick fingers were roughly shoved into her secret space. Her screams of pain were muffled by his mouth crushed against hers. She tried to tear his hand from under her skirt, pinching her knees together hard enough to dislodge his hand.

She knew she was forever tainted by the incident. A year of therapy had done little to help her evade the nightmares, the memory, and the repulsive feelings she had toward any intimate contact. It was hard to hold Michael's hand, even if it warmed her ice-cold fingers.

Could she pull this off? Could she trust Michael's word, both verbal and written?

His voice reached her. "Caroline?"

She stared at him, searching the depths of his eyes with her own. She hadn't missed that he'd promised to protect her. If nothing else, he could protect her from the monster. "Yes?" she whispered.

He turned her away from Mr. Paulson and whispered softly in her ear, "Do you still want to go through with this?"

She didn't look at him, but she nodded. Turning back to stand before the JP, she asked, "What am I to say?"

Mr. Paulson's look softened. He must have taken her reluctance as a case of nerves. He said the phrases, and Caroline repeated slowly, "I, Caroline Rose Perret, take you, Michael Henry DuBois, to be my husband. To have and to hold from this day forward, for better or for worse, for richer—" She paused, "for poorer, in sickness and in health. I promise to love, honor, cherish, and protect you all the days of my life, until death do us part."

Mr. Paulson turned to Michael. "May I have the rings?"

Michael's expression mirrored how she felt: stricken. In the haste of the morning, they had forgotten to get rings.

Mr. And Mrs. Paulson both chuckled. "It's not unusual to forget the rings. We'll just move on then," the justice of the peace said.

"It is my privilege, and with the authority given by the State of Vermont and the Town of Haston, I now pronounce you husband and wife. You may now seal the vow with a kiss."

Michael and Caroline stared at each other. The ending kiss was another thing they hadn't discussed.

"Aww, come on now. It's okay. We'll step out to give you some privacy." Mrs. Paulson winked as she grasped her husband's arm and steered him toward the door.

CHAPTER TWENTY-EIGHT

Alone in the room, they stood still, eyes locked, her hand in his.

"May I kiss you?" Michael asked. "Just this once?"

Caroline considered the request. Since the incident, she had only been kissed by two men. First, Randy, the ex-boyfriend who kidnapped her in a run for the Canadian border. His kisses had been sultry and insistent. She was so infatuated with him that she had let him have her virginity. That first time should have been magical. Instead, it hurt considerably. She had heard the first time was painful. But the pain never went away. He did things to her body she would never have imagined. Letting him have his way with her was something she regretted deeply as he became more demanding ,controlling and hurtful.

The second was David. He was fine with her chaste pecks and her demands to put off any intimacy, believing her a virgin, until after their wedding. As she found out after the wedding was canceled, he was never interested in her. Only her money mattered, and he would comply with whatever she asked to get it.

Caroline steeled herself for the mashing of Michael's lips against hers before nodding her consent.

He closed the tiny space between them, not letting go of her hands, rubbing a thumb lightly across her knuckles. His eyes bore into hers with softness a moment before he leaned forward and brushed his lips against hers. They lingered there, light, soft, warm, and non-threatening.

Caroline's mind exploded with the sensation of it. He turned his head slightly, lightening the pressure. Her toes curled, and she pressed into his kiss.

Michael's body reeled with the electric current running through him from the joining of their lips. He hadn't expected her to lean in for more. She had been so adamant about intimacy being something they would not, under any circumstances, share. Arousal stirred within him as his heart raced. He dared not go further, so he brushed across her lips before backing away. Their kiss told him much about Caroline. Despite all he assumed and the tabloids reported, Caroline was inexperienced in kissing. And if she were inexperienced in that, how many other ways was she still a virgin? He was determined to tread very lightly so as not to frighten her.

Mrs. Paulson returned just then. "Your table is waiting at the restaurant next door. Unless you'd like to postpone dinner." She gave them another wink.

Michael replied. "We'll be right over."

Their dinner was delicious. The post and beam barn, with huge stone hearth ablaze, felt intimate despite being one open structure except for the kitchen at the back of the barn. Caroline ate little of her duck breast with sautéed Swiss chard, golden beets, and mashed sweet potatoes. The last thing she wanted to do was spill or drip something on her cashmere sweater. Then she remembered that with this marriage, she could afford to replace it hundreds of times over if it were ruined.

Michael had dug into his lamb with cheddar risotto, roasted carrots, and onions with sage. Unlike her picking, he devoured his food like he hadn't eaten in days.

The whole evening was anti-climactic. At first, both of them seemed stunned into silence over what had transpired. Caroline thought it unusual. They always talked. Or argued over something while together. The event—the kiss—hung between them like a gossamer spider web. Would it trap them in its sticky threads? Or would they continue as before? Caroline didn't know. Her mind lingered on the questions.

"Tell me about your family." She fingered her wineglass, her meal unfinished.

Michael looked up, a surprised look on his face. Recovering, he said, "My father, you knew. My mother was sort of a stay-at-home mother. I'm the eldest, then there's Pamela, Alan, and Jason."

Summoning her polite conversational skills, she continued the inquiry, "Tell me about your siblings and your home life." She had always had a curiosity about the lives of the less fortunate. It must have differed from her own, but she had no idea how.

"Pamela finished at University of Vermont in December with a degree in Dietetics. She's doing her internship at UVM Medical Center." Michael sipped his wine before continuing, "Alan you've met. He's graduating high school in just a few weeks. He's been accepted to Harvard." He leaned forward as if telling her a secret. "Don't tell him I said so, but he's the smartest of all of us. His future looks bright." Sitting back in his chair, he frowned. "Jason is a little tougher to explain. He has another two years of high school. Dad's death hit him especially hard. He used to be interested in club events at school. But he's dropped out of many since then, and his grades have dropped too." Michael fingered his napkin. "I'm hoping it's temporary."

She nodded, acknowledging his words. "What about you? Your dad proudly told me you went to UMass for accounting."

"I did. When I graduated, I got a job at Stowe Winter Resorts. It was great while it lasted."

Caroline cocked her head. "You got laid off?"

Michael shook his head, his eyes closed momentarily. "No. Dad was struggling at the office. He asked me to come help him." He shrugged. "What could I say? He paid for my education. It wasn't long after the doctors figured out he was terminally ill."

"I'm so sorry." And she meant it. She'd liked Henry. In the short time he had been her accountant, she couldn't help thinking how much nicer he was than her own father. *Time to change the subject.* "Do you ski?"

"I do, or rather, I did. I haven't had much time since I started working. It's funny you get a discount on season tickets working there in corporate, but little time to use them. Do you ski?"

"Love it." Caroline smiled. At last, something they had in common.

"We'll have to go sometime this winter. I don't have any gear though."

Caroline smiled. "You'll have money to buy it now." She paused as the waitress took their plates away. "Tell me about your family life." She watched as Michael's face filled with stress, like he was experiencing mild pain. "Or not."

He shrugged. "It wasn't ideal. My dad was always at work. My mom got involved with this cat rescue association. It started with us fostering a pregnant cat and raising the kittens to an adoptable age. After that, we always had cats in the house. Except by then, my mother was involved in caring for the shelter animals. It was a volunteer position, but it consumed her." At the blank stare on Caroline's face, he added, "Did you have any pets?"

"Gosh, no. My mother thought they were dirty and revolting."

He nodded. "That's too bad. Some of my childhood confidants were the numerous cats hanging around the house. Right now, we have two. Casper and Cheese." He chuckled.

Caroline joined him. "Who gave them those names?" She giggled into her palm.

He watched her laughing. The sound thrilled him, as did the flush of her cheeks. They had been too pale all day, especially during the ceremony. "The shelter people, I think. Mom never let us change them." He leaned forward conspiratorially. "But we kids had all kinds of nicknames for them." Michael winked and sat back.

Caroline giggled again. Michael decided he could never tire of the sound.

"It sounds like an ideal childhood." Her demeanor changed. A worry line deepened on her forehead.

He scowled. " Not really. My parents weren't home much and rarely together, except at night. But even then, they kept separate bedrooms. We kids had the run of the house and yard. It was a big yard with a forest beyond the property line. We played in every inch of both. Being outside all day after school and all weekend was the norm, weather permitting. It was clear early on we were to be out of the house and keep ourselves occupied. No organized playdates or sports for us. All my friends did Boy Scouts or little league. I never had the opportunity." He grimaced with a noticeable tick in his jaw.

The dining room was all but empty as their server offered coffee and dessert. They both declined, but neither made a move to leave. Caroline's shoulders tensed as their night together in the same bed loomed ahead. Would sharing the queen-sized bed unravel all their plans?

"What about your childhood?" Michael asked.

Caroline's jaw tightened. "Like what?"

"I don't know. What was it like to be Senator Perret's daughter? Live in a mansion, in luxury?"

She closed her eyes, forcing away the most distinct memory from her childhood. "I went to private boarding schools. I had no friends," she shrugged, "which probably explains why I like to have so many around me now."

Michael's lips pressed together briefly before he asked, "Did you have any hobbies or interests?"

She thought for a minute. "No. I did homework or read books. Did everything I was told, actually. I saw what happened to Tony when he tried straying from our father's dictates. It wasn't pretty." She remembered the sight of Tony's face after the dining room incident so long ago. His purple-red and swollen face, the result of her father's fist.

"Did you have chores or ..." Michael seemed unable to voice what he was asking.

"No chores. I tried to help in the kitchen when I was very young. My mother put a stop to that. I was forbidden from doing anything. It wasn't 'proper for a lady' according to her. Everything was done for us. A team of servants took care of everything no matter which house we were in. They traveled everywhere we went. Including on our vacations, domestic or international."

"That must have cost a small fortune." Michael's amazed look made Caroline feel odd.

"I guess so. Money was not anything we ever worried about," Caroline admitted.

Michael blinked as if not knowing what to say. He gulped down the last of his wine. "Let's get the suitcases."

They escaped to her Mustang, where Michael struggled with the two suitcases belonging to her, while she carried his small duffle bag. Her pulse raced with the unknown evening ahead in their shared room, their shared bed. Would it be crass to ask Michael to sleep on the floor? Considering all he'd done to help her access her money, the thought felt extraordinarily out of order.

The room was cozy, with the ever-present fire burning low in the grate. The bed had been turned down, exposing white sheets and four fluffy down pillows. The tray on top of the bureau held two crystal flutes and a demi-bottle of champagne. Extra blankets and pillows sat on shelves in the closet. While Michael opened the champagne and poured it, Caroline inspected the rest of the large room. The bathroom was tiled and simply decorated, with a walk-in shower and a pedestal soaking tub. Caroline sighed at the pleasurable thought of slipping into hot water perfumed with the bath bombs on the vanity. If she stayed there long enough, would Michael fall asleep?

When she returned to the bedroom area, Michael handed her the crystal flute. "To us."

Caroline nodded and gulped down the Veuve Clicquot. She set down the glass. "I'm exhausted."

Michael nodded hesitantly, as if he expected more from her. As she ignored him, he hoisted his duffle onto the bed.

Wordlessly, they each got out toiletries and night clothes.

"You go first," Caroline suggested.

"Are you sure?" Michael asked. "I can wait."

She shook her head. "I want to take a hot bath. It's been an emotional day."

Michael gave her a quick half-nod before disappearing behind the bathroom door. The shower was on in minutes; the sound of the water beating against the glass enclosure.

Caroline laid her suitcase on the bed and opened it. When she saw the silken negligee, her breath caught in her throat. She hadn't anticipated sharing a room tonight or any night of their "honeymoon." The revealing nature of the negligee was not something she wanted Michael to see in case he got the wrong idea.

There was no other option unless she wanted to sleep in jeans. *I can slip under the covers if I wait until he's asleep before coming out of the bathroom.* She fussed with laying out her clothes for tomorrow as a distraction for her unsettled nerves. Tomorrow's journey would be a six hour ride from Haston to Mount Desert Island. That didn't include a few stops along the way for beverages, food, or bio-breaks. Finished with her arranging, she sat in one of the wing chairs in front of the fireplace and trolled through social media.

The bathroom door opened, releasing a cloud of steam. Michael stepped out, half-naked, a towel wrapped around his lower torso.

Caroline gasped. She had never imagined he'd have a set of eight-pack abs and a solid chest. Even his arms were muscular, as though he worked out often lifting weights. His usual business attire in the office concealed much from her eyes. Much they were now appreciating far more than she would have thought.

He stopped short at her stare, his face turning crimson. "I—I forgot my pajamas." Without another word, he snatched them up from the bedside table and disappeared back into the bathroom.

Minutes later, he returned in navy pin-striped pajama bottoms, toweling his hair dry. "It's all yours."

All mine? Her eyes didn't stray from his ripped physique. It made perfect sense he'd sleep without a top, considering the warmth of the room and the early summer heat. "I'll be a while." She picked up her things and escaped to the bathroom. She'd stay in that bathwater until her teeth were chattering just to make sure Michael was fast asleep when she emerged.

CHAPTER TWENTY-NINE

Caroline picked up her cell phone and called Rachel once she was safely in the soothing hot water. "Hey girlfriend, how are you? How's the cop?"

"I'm so glad you called. I have so much to tell you," Rachel said. "First, I'm not seeing Patrick anymore."

"What? I thought you said he was the one?"

"He is, or was. But you know how it is. Our social standing has to be protected. I let him down easy. I started dating another guy. He's handsome and wealthy, *and* he's going to Dartmouth med school."

"But do you love him?" Caroline couldn't explain why that suddenly mattered. In the socialite world, it wasn't a matter of love. Couples joined forces to reach higher social levels. "Are you sure about Patrick? You said he treated you like a princess."

Rachel sighed into the phone. "He did. I can't deny that. But Merrick's parents have lots of money and a huge compound in the Hamptons. They dine with the governor of New York. And he's good enough for me."

Caroline bit her lip. "If you say so." She held her tongue, then changed her mind. "I would think you'd want someone who truly cared and loved you rather than Mr. Rich Guy."

"I like him. That's good enough for me." Rachel started sniffling. "I thought you'd be happy for me. I want you to be in my wedding."

"Has Merrick proposed already?"

"Not in so many words, but he talks about our future together. I think it's a done deal even without an engagement ring yet."

The bathwater was getting chilly. "I'm happy you are happy. Just don't make a hasty decision. Money isn't everything."

"What? I can't believe you just said that!"

Caroline needed to get out of the water. "Look, my bathwater has gone cold. I'll talk to you later, okay?"

"But I wanted to hear what's happening with you? That creep hasn't been stalking you or anything, has he?"

Caroline stood up in the soaker tub. "No. I'm going out of town for a few weeks to try to shake him off. The cellular service is sketchy there, so I'll call when I get back." Her toes were freezing. "I've got to go. I'll call you later. Bye." She disconnected the call and began her nightly pre-bedtime ritual.

Michael waited, flipping through a variety of books on the mantel. He selected a John Le Carre novel he'd read long ago, settled himself by the fire, and began reading. Or so it looked. His mind kept wandering to the woman behind the bathroom door. A sigh, a splash of water, and her voice interrupted his concentration several times before he gave up. She must have been on the phone with Tony. He closed the book and let it drop to the carpet beside his chair. Resting his head back, he released his mind from the day's events and let it dissolve into sleep.

A floral scent tickled his nose, awakening him. He opened his eyes to see the goddess who was now his wife, if in name only. She had gathered her flaxen hair into a ponytail, the golden strands cascading down her back like a waterfall. Wrapped in the complimentary terry cloth bath robe, she reminded him of a butterfly ready to escape its cocoon confinement. "Are you feeling better?"

With a shy smile, she nodded and went to the side of the bed. "I'm better. I'm going to sleep." And turning her back to him, she removed the bathrobe. "Turn around," she demanded. "I hadn't expected us to share a room tonight. I brought the wrong nightgown."

Michael did as she requested but couldn't help but steal a look over his shoulder.

His breath caught in his lungs. Her lithe figure was draped in a long silk, pearly pink nightgown. Creamy white lace slits down the sides of her legs gave him a glimpse of their firmness and length as

QUEST FOR LOVE

she walked to the bed, the sheerness of the fabric outlining the thong beneath. Slipping her delicate feet under the bed linens, her front upper torso faced him. Only lace covered her breasts, revealing hardened nipples. Was it the chill after the hot bath that did it? He tried diverting his thoughts to something mundane, but his body's reaction became evident. His cock responded furiously, tenting his pajama bottoms as he sat in the chair. He folded his hands together and pressed down as inconspicuously as he could. He had to sleep beside this beautiful woman and not touch her?

"I think I'll sleep here," he said as much to himself as to her. He rose to get a blanket from the closet shelf, settled back in the wing chair, and closed his eyes. *I can't watch.*

The bedside lamp clicked off, and he listened intently as she drifted off and her breathing slowed to a steady, soft rhythm.

Sleep evaded him. His thoughts were on the fairy princess sleeping in the bed before him. After dozing a few times, he awoke to find her thrashing in the bed, her vocalizations filled with fear, her groans and stifled mewing making it clear she was having a bad dream.

He went to her side of the bed and turned on the lamp. Without touching her, he whispered, "Caroline, it's alright. Wake up. I'm here."

She startled upright, her eyes ablaze with fear, her hands clutching the bed sheet to her breasts. Seeing him, she screamed.

He backed away, his index finger to his lips, trying to silence her from screaming again. "It's me, Michael. It's okay. You're safe."

A hard knock on the bedroom door interrupted them. Michael opened the door a crack. It was Mr. Paulson. "Everything okay in here?" His voice was stern, his features tense.

"Yes, she was having a nightmare." Michael let the man step just inside the door to ascertain Caroline's safety.

When she saw him, she said, "I'm so sorry. I had this t-terrifying nightmare. Truly, I'm fine."

Mr. Paulson nodded at her before giving him a glare. "My apologies for intruding. Good night."

Michael returned to the bedside. "Is there anything I can do? A glass of water, a warm face towel?"

"No! I'm okay. I'll be okay."

He wasn't sure if she was trying to convince him or herself. "I'm right here if you need me." He started back to the chair.

"No. You—" She stared at him. "Sleep here." She rubbed her palm across the top sheet, seeking to leave it between her body and his. "It might bring it back, but I'm willing to take the chance."

Michael nodded and slipped into the far side of the bed. He settled down just as Caroline shut off the lamp. With his back to her, he murmured, "Good night, Caroline."

"Good night, Michael."

They were both silent a few minutes before Michael heard her say, "Thank you."

"Welcome," he whispered over his shoulder. Her phrase ignited questions. How would sleeping beside her bring back her nightmare? Before he could thoroughly ponder the question, he fell into a deep sleep.

Caroline awoke, lying on her side, facing the shaded windows. The sunny morning seeped around the shades' edges, lighting the room in a dim glow. For a few seconds, she forgot where she was. When her memory clicked in, she propped herself up on her elbow and looked at the fireplace. The only sign of the previous night's fire was the pile of ash under the iron grate. The chair in front of the hearth was empty. *Where's Michael? Did he bale out during the night?*

"I'm here," he murmured as if reading her thoughts, the heat of his breath tickling her ear.

QUEST FOR LOVE

Caroline twisted toward his voice, finding him lying beside her on the bed. "What are you doing here?"

"You invited me. After your nightmare," he replied before retreating to the bathroom.

The memory of it crawled back to her mind like a stink bug. Unbidden and unwelcome. The recurring nightmare from her childhood, Mr. Paulson at the door, Michael covering for her. She had invited him to sleep on the bed beside her.

A robed Michael emerged from the bathroom and approached the bed. "How did you sleep?"

Brushing a lock of hair out of her eyes, she answered, "Okay, I guess." She saw him check his watch. "What time is it?"

"Nearly eight-thirty. We should get some breakfast before the pub closes." He gestured toward the bathroom. "Ladies first?"

Nodding, Caroline flung back the covers and reached for her robe.

Michael's throat thickened at the sight of this woman in her silky nightgown. Caroline sat on the edge of the bed, her hair tousled, her skin flushed with warmth. Or was it nerves?

The blush on her face made him avert his eyes. He walked to the fireplace, picked up the poker, and jabbed at the ashes as if looking for warmth. The sight of gorgeous Caroline had him steaming with desire. He would have opened a window, but it was probably already hot outside.

His senses on alert, he felt the air swish about him as she passed. The fragrance of last night's bubble bath tickled his nose. The two sensations, along with the vision of her, raised goosebumps. When she opened the bathroom door, he glanced her way, catching a glimpse of a firm bottom. She hadn't put on her robe after all. Her arms clutched clothing in front of her torso instead. His cock went rigid.

To his surprise, she didn't dally. Neither did he. While she was behind the door, he quickly changed into a polo shirt and a fresh pair of jeans. Caroline emerged dressed in tight-fitting jeans and an off-the-shoulder jersey.

When she walked past him, his hand brushed her arm. She turned to him, her eyes wide with what looked like fear. "I'm sorry. I can't ignore what happened last night. Are you sure you're okay? Would you like to talk about it?"

With a tight shake of her head, Caroline headed for her suitcase, stuffed the nightgown and toiletries bag inside, and closed it. "No. It was all the stress of the day. There's nothing more to discuss. Let's go. I need some coffee." She sauntered past him, heading for the door.

CHAPTER THIRTY

The ride to MDI went well enough. Their six-hour trip turned into seven and one-half as they stopped twice, once for lunch and a grocery store stop in Ellsworth.

The Hannaford's was enormous. Far bigger than any grocery store Caroline had ever been in. Then again, she hadn't started grocery shopping routinely until she lost her maid. Walking beside the shopping cart, she stopped to examine an item. It was a new kind of breakfast bar with fifty grams of protein. Intrigued, she dropped the item in the cart.

"Hey!" Michael called out as she walked away.

The tone of his voice sounded angry. She turned back just as he was placing the box back on the shelf. "We're here for real food. Not over-processed junk."

Planting her hands on her hips, she walked back to the cart. "Don't I get to have what I want?" She lifted the box and put it back in the cart.

"Not while you can't afford to pay the bill." Michael took it out again.

"You're the reason I don't have any money to buy my own items."

His right eyebrow rose. "Let's not get into that here." He held out the box again. "Look at this label." He scanned the back of the box. "It says here there's forty-five grams of sugar in each two-ounce bar. That's outrageous. How is that even possible?" He held the box up along with his other hand as if asking God.

"But I like them. Besides, I need the protein in my diet." Caroline snatched it from him and stared at the nutritional content chart. "How do you read this thing?"

Michael gave her a quick lesson on reading the chart. After the lesson ended, he picked up a different box and showed her how to compare the labels. He held up the second box. "This may only have thirty grams of protein, but the sugar content is less than five grams."

He dropped the box into the cart. "It's better for you, and it's cheaper." He pointed to the shelf labels with the prices.

"Huh." Caroline put the fifty-grams-of-protein box back on the shelf. "I never knew about that label." Michael's demonstration shocked her. She never thought to look at the nutritional information or the price label.

Pressing ahead, Michael said, "Let's get some fresh fruits and vegetables and breakfast foods. We'll be eating most of our meals out anyway." He started forward again. "What do you like to cook?"

"I don't cook. It's not my forte."

Michael glared at her again. "What have you been eating? One hundred dollars couldn't last all week, even for takeout." He knew she didn't do fast food or anything that wasn't unhealthy.

Caroline shrugged. "I had a freezer full of food the maid would make ahead of time whenever I wanted it. Plus, there's always granola or kefir smoothies."

Michael's eyes rolled. "I see. I guess I'm going to be doing the cooking."

The rest of the shopping trip went at a snail's pace. Caroline stopped to check and compare the nutritional labels on lots of items. "Caroline, we're wasting time here. Grab some eggs, and let's check out."

She stared at the varieties of eggs, unsure which to choose jumbo, large, extra-large, medium, free-range, cage-free, and omega-3-fortified. As Michael glared at her, she placed the cage-free, omega-3-fortified, organic eggs into the cart.

He shook his head violently. "No. Large regular eggs. We don't need fancy eggs."

"But I want these." She wheeled around, her eyes fiery, and glared at him. Her hands jerked to her hips again, and she stamped her foot.

"No." Michael laughed. "Love the temper tantrum bit. So do the other shoppers." He glanced past her to see a few shoppers laughing at her antics. "Reminds me of my neighbors' three-year-old."

Caroline glanced about, noticing the attention her little scene had attracted. Heat flooded her face. "Great. Let's get out of here," she said, her voice dripping with sarcasm.

After checking out, Michael steered the cart to the Mustang and placed the half dozen bags on the back seat. "Mind if I drive?" He gave Caroline a hopeful look. She gave him a long, hard stare.

Just before he was going to say, "Never mind," she held out the keys.

"Be very careful," she said, narrowing her eyes.

It worked out well. With him driving, Caroline could read aloud the directions to the house, which she had been advised to print out in case the cell service was sketchy.

When they crossed over the Trenton Bridge, the only bridge to the island, Michael flashed a wide grin. "I can't believe how relieved I feel. Just getting away from the office." He stopped at the traffic light.

"We take a left here to stop at the National Park office and pay," Caroline advised. "When was your last vacation?"

Michael thought about it for a minute. It felt like another lifetime ago. Long before his father got sick. "I think there was one long weekend during my Stowe job. That was pretty much it since I graduated from UMass."

"What about spring breaks?"

"One must have money to travel during spring break," he reminded her dryly.

"Where did you go on your long weekend?" Caroline pointed for them to take a right at the vee in the road. "Any place special?"

Michael said, "I didn't go far. I went up to Montreal for a four-day weekend.

"I've always wanted to go there."

"It was great fun. The weather was beautiful, and the basilica and the botanical gardens were gorgeous. And the food! I never ate such good food in my life, and I haven't since."

"Turn here. The office is just there." She pointed to her right.

Caroline was waiting for him when he got out of the car and crossed to her side of the vehicle. She held out her open palm.

"Aww, that's all I get?" Michael pouted like a spoiled child.

"That's all for now," Caroline said, pocketing the keys he dropped into her hand.

"Maybe another time?" Michael wiggled his eyebrows suggestively.

"Don't count on it." Caroline chuckled. "This is my baby, and no one else, not even Tony, has ever driven it."

Back on the road with their admission paid, they headed west along Route 102 to the quieter side of the island. They passed a roadside food truck. Caroline pulled into the parking lot.

"What's up?" Michael shot her a questioning look.

"I thought we could pick up some dinner to go. It's well past seven."

It made sense. Michael wasn't going to feel up to cooking anything, and Caroline didn't cook at all. They made their choices, and Michael paid for it.

Back on the road, Caroline steered the car through the forested wilderness.

Michael was surprised she hadn't picked a location on the east side of the Somes Sound or in downtown Bar Harbor itself for more excitement and shopping adventures.

He decided to ask outright. "I'm surprised we're heading west. I would have thought you would pick a luxurious place closer to Bar Harbor."

"I do like Bar Harbor. But the last time I came here with friends for two weeks, we sorta got kicked out of our hotel for being too noisy and drunk. I thought booking a rental house in the woods on the west side would prevent that fiasco from happening again."

"I didn't know you ran with such a rowdy bunch."

Her head bobbed left and right. "It depends on who's in the company. Some of those people wouldn't have been invited this time."

He probed a little further. "But why do you always travel within a pack, taking everyone along yet footing the bill everywhere you go?"

She glanced over at him. "They're my friends. Don't you take your friends with you on vacation?"

He grunted. "No. I haven't had much time for vacations, but I certainly wouldn't ask hangers-on to join me *and* pay their entire way." He tried to bite his tongue, but the question popped out. "So, where are your 'friends' now that you need them? Or are they no longer friends because they can't mooch off your generosity anymore."

The tires screeched as she pulled the car off to the side of the narrow road. She slammed the gear shift in neutral and turned to him with a furious glare. "Look. You're the one who put a kibosh on this trip. You put me on a budget. Cut up my credit cards. You're the one who stopped me from inviting friends along."

He raked his fingers through his hair. "I did. I put you on a budget because you couldn't stop spending money you no longer had on your so called friends." His face flushed with indignation. She liked to make it sound like *he* was the problem. When would she take responsibility for her own actions? "How many of them offered to fund the rest of the trip or even offered to share the cost?"

"None." Her reply sounded like a growl coming from deep in her chest.

"Do they still consider you a friend, or have they moved on to deeper pockets?" He knew he was being cruel, but he couldn't hold back his assessment of the situation any longer.

She turned away as if looking in her side mirror. Her right shoulder heaved. When it did it again, he knew she was crying. He hated himself for it. He hated trying to make it clear that those weren't friends. They were followers sucking up as much from her as they could get. And they didn't care a damn about Caroline without her money.

"I'm sorry. I shouldn't have pressed you." When she didn't respond he added, "I just want you to see that they're moochers. They'll try to come back into your good graces when the trust fund gets dispersed. My question to you is, why do you encourage this dependency, and are you going to accept them back when they realize you're loaded again?"

She whipped her head around, eyes red and swollen, tears streaking her face. "That's none of your business!"

"Oh, but it is. You owe me one million dollars. I want to make sure I collect it before you blow the rest of your inheritance. We're married now." He wanted to shake her, wake her up to the facts.

"So you'll call out my friends for being moochers, but you haven't looked in the mirror? Aren't you getting something out of this relationship too?" She sputtered, her hands wiping away the surge of tears that dripped off her face.

"It was your idea. Remember?" He was tired of arguing. Tired of being in this damn car. "Can we get to the house? I'm exhausted, you're exhausted. Let's discuss this later."

Her aching head dropped to her chest. It had been Caroline's idea, yet Michael had paid for everything so far. The marriage license, the wedding package, groceries, dinner, even gas for her car. She wanted to blame him for freezing her accounts and canceling her credit cards but knew he'd done so to protect her.

The things he had said made her feel utterly alone. Only Rachel remained despite everything she had done with and for her friends. The rumors of her insolvency had spread through her crowd like wildfire. How they had found out, she didn't know. Perhaps Rachel's loose lips had let the facts be known. Not one of her so-called friends had called to offer help or even a kind word.

She put the car in gear and eased it back onto the road. The house wasn't far ahead and she was antsy to get out of this confined space, find the opposite end of the house from Michael and forget he was even there.

They arrived at the address given for the house. As they rolled up the driveway through woods on either side of the road, she wondered what the house would look like. She'd only seen pictures on the website. It was a classic two-story colonial from the front, but two identical two-story wings jutted out toward the back of the building. Each wing held two bedrooms, one smaller and narrow along the outside of the wing, while a large bedroom with an ensuite bath was at the end on each level. The space between the two wings held a beautifully landscaped patio. Both functional and reclusive in feel, it held several outdoor dining sets, a huge stone grilling section, and a small dipping pool. The owner had warned them the pool had not yet been set up as the weather was still unpredictable for mid-May.

Handling one of her suitcases, Caroline picked out the spacious end room on the left wing. "I like this room."

"Sure," Michael said, hefting her heavier suitcase on the luggage stand beside the closet. "I'll take the one above you."

CHAPTER THIRTY-ONE

The succulent smell of bacon frying woke Caroline from a light sleep. Her night had been difficult. Sleep had evaded her until after midnight and only stayed periodically until dawn's first light. She paused on the edge of the bed, debating the real need to get up. The aroma of fresh coffee mingling with the bacon tempted her to hasten to the kitchen. Did a cook come with the house rental after all? She slipped on her robe and ventured in the direction of the smell causing her stomach to growl in a very unladylike manner.

The hallway opened to a large kitchen with a cathedral ceiling. Michael stood before the stove, some flat black utensil in his hand, white apron ties wrapped around his waist and neck. He turned around to display a white apron adorned with a red lobster covering his polo shirt and blue jeans. "Ah, there you are. The bacon, home fries, and coffee are ready. How do you like your eggs, my dear?"

The surprise on her face must have hit Michael where it hurt. "What?" He looked down at his attire. "Is something wrong?"

"You can make breakfast?" She sauntered closer to inspect the various pans on the stove. "I don't eat breakfast."

"Well, you should. You could use some meat on those bones you carry around." He paused. When she didn't respond, he asked, "Toast instead?"

"Didn't we buy yogurt and kefir and fresh blueberries?" She opened the refrigerator and searched.

"We did. But there isn't a blender." He turned away when a burning smell returned his attention to the skillets. He removed the bacon to a paper towel-lined plate and turned off all the burners. "I searched already."

Caroline sighed, removing the blueberries and plain yogurt from the fridge. "I'll have this."

QUEST FOR LOVE

"Suit yourself." He re-lit the gas burner and cooked himself two scrambled eggs. He placed them on his plate along with a spoonful of home fries and toast. He brought the platter of bacon and set it in the center of the table. Once settled, he grabbed three slices of crispy bacon, took a bite of one slice, and moaned, "Mmm, so good. I love crispy bacon."

"It will do no good to entice me to eat something so unhealthy." She spooned a heap of yogurt over the berries in her bowl and stirred. Her eyes were drawn to the plate of the bacon as she stirred and stirred. It had been quite some time since she'd indulged in a slice.

Michael continued to eat, humming to himself and groaning with exuberance while chewing his bacon.

She knew he was baiting her. *Still, one piece* ... She dropped her spoon into the bowl with a clatter. "One piece can't hurt."

Michael bit back his smile as he spread jam over a slice of toast. "No, one piece will not harm you. Or your figure." He gave the plate a shove closer to her end of the table.

Caroline stood and reached for the closest slice. The end was in her mouth before her butt was back in her chair. Enchanted, her eyes closed. The taste was better than she remembered.

"There're two more slices I cooked for you. If you don't want them—" He reached for the plate, but she scooped up the remaining slices. "You want me to make you an egg?"

"No, thank you. This is enough." She gobbled up the slices, lingering on the last mouthful before opening her eyes. "I ...um, I don't cook because I don't know how to." She spooned some of the healthy yogurt and fruit mix into her mouth, pinched her lips together, and gave Michael a fake smile.

"I can teach you while we're here. One thing each day." He looked at her with a sideways glance. "I assume you know how to make toast."

"Of course, I know how to make toast."

"Great, that's one thing off the list." He changed the topic when she didn't rise to the bait. "I was thinking we should explore the island today. Perhaps downtown Bar Harbor?"

"I don't have any money to buy things."

"Have you never window-shopped? Looked but not indulged in purchasing?"

She raised her eyes to heaven as if thinking before saying, "No. Never."

Michael rose from the table, heading for the sink with his empty plate. "I guess you are going to learn something new." He placed the dirty dishes in the dishwasher and wiped the countertop and stove clean. As if feeling her eyes burning into his back, he turned around and caught her making a face at him. "Shall we meet here at ten o'clock and head out? Perhaps we can have a light lunch in town."

"You're buying, I presume. Since I don't have any money."

He nodded and gave her a sheepish smile. "Until that money is released, yes."

She pondered the proposition. "Fine."

"Great." He strode for the hallway that led to the stairs to the second floor. "See you then." He yelled back over his shoulder, "Wear sensible shoes."

Michael let her linger in the shops, but if she picked something up and approached him to ask for money, he would purse his lips and shake his head. It was a good thing her credit cards were frozen and her bank account unavailable. Otherwise, she would have depleted it all after their two-hour tour.

Walking back to finish their loop on the other side of the road, Michael reached for her hand.

Caroline pulled it away and glared at him. "No intimacy."

"Holding someone's hand is not intimate. Besides, if anyone recognizes you and takes a picture, don't we need to look like a newly married happy couple?"

She glared at him again before conceding. "Fine. But only when we're out in public." She held out her hand.

Michael grasped it. The feeling of his soft palm and the slim length of his long fingers gave her goosebumps. Holding hands with a handsome man wasn't so bad. A handsome husband. *God, I can't believe he's now my husband.* Just thinking the words sent a thrill coursing through her body. He squeezed her hand and gestured toward a bookstore across the street. Her heart thudded faster as the warmth from his palm against hers spread up her arm.

On the way back to the house, Caroline confessed, "That was difficult."

"Walking hand in hand?"

Shaking her head, she said, "No. Not that. Not being able to buy anything." *And dealing with all the feelings holding your hand brought up.*

"Ah, but isn't it satisfying to know you can admire the goods and still walk away."

"Huh. I'm not so sure about that." She squinted at him, giving him a skeptical look before pulling into the driveway. Suddenly, Caroline wished they'd never made a contract. Something about this man stirred up her insides like no one else had. It was different from her infatuation with Randy. That fiery lust had been carefully orchestrated by Randy to snare her. This...this thing she felt for Michael was a slow burn full of tiny moments of sparks like flint against a pocket knife.

"Perhaps we can forgo another non-shopping trip tomorrow and go for an easy hike on a carriage road instead," Michael suggested.

Caroline laughed. "Hah! A walk on a dirt road? I'm sure I can find something better to do than that. Like read a book."

"The trees have leafed out, and some of the roads lead to scenic lakes and ponds. It'll be beautiful." He cocked his head and gave her a quizzical look. "A walk is far better for you than sitting on your arse reading all afternoon."

"We'll discuss it in the morning. Shall we?" Caroline got out of the car and entered the house.

CHAPTER THIRTY-TWO

The next morning, Michael tapped lightly on her bedroom door. "Wakey time." The phrase came to him from his earlier years trying to get his siblings up for school. Especially Jason, who often needed to be physically dragged, kicking and crying from his bed.

"What do you want?" Caroline's groggy voice called through the door. "Is the house on fire?"

"Not yet, but I'm starting breakfast. If you want to eat cold leftovers, that's your prerogative, but personally, I like my omelet hot." He strode away to the kitchen.

When she hadn't shown up by the time the coffee finished brewing, he returned to the door and knocked again. "Coffee's ready."

The door flung open. Caroline wore shorts and a Chanel tee shirt. "I'm coming," she grumbled.

Michael's throat thickened at the sight of her long lovely legs. Realizing he was staring, he tore his eyes away and spied her unmade bed. "You didn't make your bed."

She leaned against the door frame. "My maid always made the bed. And the food. Which is why I don't know how to do either."

"It's simple. Let me show you." Michael strode past her into the room and described how to make a bed in patient detail.

Caroline watched from a distance, offering no help as he explained. When he stepped back, presenting the finished product with a flourish, she clapped. "Wonderful, but what's the point? I'm just going to climb back in tonight," she said dryly, turning on her bare heels and heading for the kitchen.

Michael followed, undeterred. "I'll help you make it tomorrow."

"Great," she deadpanned.

After breakfast, Michael eyed the cereal bowl Caroline had left on the counter next to her empty coffee mug. "If you were here with your friends, who would do the cooking and cleaning?"

"The maid service. Too bad I hadn't pre-paid for it this time."

He gestured toward the dirty dishes. "Well, we don't have a maid service. While I'm happy to do the cooking, I don't think I should clean up as well."

A flush crept up Caroline's cheeks as she thrust her chin out. "But you're the one who likes things neat."

"We're a team now. Husband and wife. We should share the responsibilities as a married couple."

She stared at him, a suspicious look on her face.

He cocked his head and gave her a look. She rolled her eyes and flounced over to the sink. "Fine," she said before rinsing her bowl and cup and putting them in the dishwasher. She even took the dishcloth and wiped down the counter.

"Thank you," he called as she headed out of the kitchen.

They walked the carriage roads to Jordan Pond, Eagle Lake, and Great Long Pond over the next four days. They also drove along the loop road, stopping to see Sand Beach, Thunder Hole, and Otter Point.

Caroline found the environment relaxing. For once, she wasn't thinking of what to do next. Rather, she was enjoying the scenery and the leisure time, having no detailed plan, no time schedule, and no urgency to move on to make someone else happy. Even Michael was non-committal about their wanderings. He paid for lunches when they were out, but no other money changed hands between them. And the simple foods were delicious. Especially the seafood, which was so fresh she could taste the ocean with every delicious bite. And he held her hand as often as she would let him. It wasn't as bad as she thought. His hands were soft, the fingers nimble, probably from all the computer time at work. Walking beside him began to feel natural, comfortable in a manner she hadn't anticipated.

QUEST FOR LOVE

Michael was relaxed and easygoing. They were able to strike up conversations, talk about everything from television series and cartoons they watched as children all the way to discussing books they had read. It was unlike any time she had ever spent in another's company. Her former friends' discussions involved gossip, expensive travel plans, spending money, or cutting down someone's reputation. What a contrast this was. Michael's and her time together was as light and refreshing as the constant breezes off the Atlantic Ocean.

On their fifth day, they were window-shopping in Bass Harbor when they overheard people on the street discussing the damage to the Trenton Bridge. During their lunch at the Seafood Ketch, they confirmed the bridge had been damaged severely by a runaway tugboat. The only way in and out of Mount Desert Island was closed to vehicular traffic. Passenger ferries were being organized to carry foot traffic back to the mainland. But vehicles would have to wait until the state could erect a temporary replacement. The governor promised the situation would be alleviated as soon as possible.

Caroline stopped to admire a shop window filled with home and kitchen goods.

"Perhaps we'll be stuck here for longer than our two weeks," Michael mused. "Hey, I need to pop into a shop across the street. Why don't you go in there and browse? I'll meet you back here in fifteen, okay?"

Michael met her in the home goods store after twenty minutes. He held a brown paper bag.

"You bought something?" Caroline asked, her hands on her hips.

"Yup. My money, my choice." He shoved it into the pocket of his windbreaker.

"Not fair." Caroline pouted.

"Never mind. Besides, it might even be a present for you," Michael teased as he caught her hand and tucked it into his elbow. They strolled down the street, checking out the other shops in the tiny village.

Later that night, they sat around the lit firepit enjoying the night sky, the evening sounds and the peace.

"When do I get my present?" Caroline asked. He knew she'd been itching to ask the question all the rest of the day.

"When it's time," Michael said confidently and they spent another peaceful hour under the stars before retiring to their separate rooms for the night.

That peace was shattered not long after midnight.

CHAPTER THIRTY-THREE

Michael jolted awake to Caroline screaming in the room below his. He didn't even bother with slippers or a bathrobe. He flew down the stairs and hallway expecting to find an intruder threatening her. Bursting into the room, he flicked on the overhead light to find her sitting up in bed, crying uncontrollably.

"What's happened?" Michael demanded.

She looked up at him, her eyes wide with fear. "N-nightmares." She grabbed her pillow and crushed it to her chest.

"Are you sure?" He searched the room, checked the windows were locked, and returned to stand beside her bed.

Still sobbing, Caroline looked forlorn, tiny, frail, and frightened out of her wits.

"Is there anything I can do?" He sat on the edge of her bed. She scrambled away from him to the opposite side of the bed. Sensing her inexplicable terror, he jumped up and backed away against the wall. "I'm sorry. I didn't mean to scare you further."

His mind reeled at her response to his physical closeness. What could possibly cause her to react so violently? And then it dawned on him. The signs added up. Poor self-esteem, inability to trust, inability to be alone comfortably, compulsive shopping, withdrawal from forming real relationships. She had been abused, possibly sexually, based on her no-intimacy clause. "I'm not going to hurt you. I just want to be sure you are okay."

The pillow clutched to her chest lowered an inch or two. She swallowed hard, but her eyes never left him. At last, she stuttered, "I-I'm ok-kay."

He nodded. "Good. I'll be out in the living room to protect you. You are safe."

"You don't have to protect me," Caroline sniffled.

"I vowed I would. And I meant it." He turned and left the room, closing the door behind him. Every bone in his body wanted to scoop her up and hug her tight to make the boogie man go away. But if his hunch was correct, that was the last thing he should do. In no way should he touch her without her direct consent. He only hoped she would understand, and yes, trust he was not going to hurt her.

Michael was already in the kitchen getting ready to make breakfast when she arrived. Neither made mention of the night's event. Caroline joined him as he set out the fixin's. "First lesson?" Michael asked.

Caroline nodded and joined him by the stove as he explained the finer points of scrambling eggs. The bacon was already crisping in another frying pan. "Today's menu includes eggs, bacon, and blueberry pancakes." He gave her some instructions about grilling pancakes as he ladled a spoonful of mix onto the hot griddle. "Coffee's ready." He jerked his head toward the full pot in the coffeemaker.

"Thanks," she whispered. She felt embarrassed by her actions and reactions last night. The very last thing she wanted to do was have her recurrent nightmare. The nightmare that started so long ago still ravaged her body and mind all these years later. She poured herself a cup and was about to sit down at the table when she realized he didn't have any. "Would you like some?"

"Thanks. I thought you'd never ask. Cream, no sugar, please."

"See here," he said, gesturing to the pancake on the griddle. "When bubbles form on top, it's time to flip." With a flourish, he scooped it up with his spatula and turned it over.

Caroline clapped. "Bravo!"

Michael bowed and then stood back, leaning against the kitchen counter, the spatula in his hand. "What are you having?"

The offering caused her stomach to grumble. It all sounded so good, but she had been overeating this entire trip. *I can lose the excess weight when I get home.* "All of it." Her hands cupped the mug, happy to have something to grasp. He moved smoothly around the kitchen and stove with practiced ease, his actions economical and confident. A smile crept over her face. "You are a multi-faceted man."

He stopped flipping pancakes to glance back at her, a smile on his face. "That I am. I've not had an easy life. The best thing I did was stop waiting for help or attention I would never get." He plated their meals and set them down on the table.

They began eating, a hesitant silence between them. He must have opened the kitchen window earlier because bird chatter filled their silent room. "What shall we do today?" she asked.

"I was hoping to do a harder hike in Acadia. Do you feel up to it?" Michael retrieved the coffeepot and gave them refills.

Thinking some more strenuous activity would help her sleep better, she replied, "Yes."

A mewing sound came from outside the kitchen door. Michael looked out the window. "We have company." He opened the door wide to reveal a skinny, brown cat with tiger stripes along its body sitting on the back stoop. It hesitated a moment before scurrying inside.

"A cat?" Caroline recoiled as the young cat rubbed up against her leg. "It might have fleas."

"It looks like it's starving." Michael snatched it up and set the cat on his lap. He picked bits of scrambled eggs off his plate and fed them to the cat. "He, or she, likes eggs." He added a tiny fragment of bacon. The cat gobbled up everything he offered, its nose in the air, sniffing for more. "Hang on, buddy, I'll make you some more." He set the cat on the floor and fried another egg in the skillet.

"You're making the cat breakfast?" Caroline asked, her question dripping with incredulity.

"Why not? It looks starved and we don't have cat food. And we have plenty of eggs." He gestured toward the eighteen-count egg carton, which was still more than three-quarters full. When it was ready, he set the plate of eggs on the floor. "Here you go, Ringo."

"Ringo? You've already named the cat Ringo?" Caroline watched the cat practically inhale the entire plate of food.

"The rings on its tail. Ringo," Michael said defiantly.

Caroline looked at the tail. Indeed, there were six darker brown rings around the cat's tail.

"Maybe you shouldn't get too attached. He could be a neighbor's cat." The cat was purring loudly, weaving between Michael's legs as it rubbed its skinny body against them.

"It'll be fine. Besides, I like cats. I have a lot of experience with them, remember?"

"I had no idea you were a cat whisperer. Suit yourself," Caroline said as she rose from the table. "I'll be getting ready to go." She left Michael sitting at the kitchen table, the cat in his arms. Caroline couldn't decide who was happier. Her feelings were chaotic. Then it dawned on her. She felt jealous of the cat.

CHAPTER THIRTY-FOUR

The Beehive loop hiking trail promised a moderate to difficult hike with the promise of spectacular views of the coastline and the islands beyond. Caroline parked the car in the Sand Beach parking lot. The hike began on a portion of the Bowl Trail. It felt exhilarating to be using her muscles. A half mile in involved ascending granite staircases and stepping on rock scrabble.

At first, she and Michael walked in single file. Some areas of the trail would not allow otherwise. But the rock scrabble was more of a problem. Caroline realized her Gucci tennis shoes were not providing as much stability for her ankles nor enough traction with the rocky surfaces. Leading, Michael would turn around and encourage her, at one point holding out his hand to assist her up the pebble-strewn granite slope. Caroline ignored it. She didn't want to touch him. Holding his hand was getting far too familiar. And it felt too nice. She had to stop it where she could.

At one overlook, they stopped to let a large group of teenagers and a family pass. Michael dug into his day pack for water bottles and fruit. They munched in silence, each lost in their own thoughts. Vacation Michael was an interesting juxtaposition to Work Michael. Back in his accounting office, he was all control, uptight, and demanding that she understand the ramifications of her financial actions and realities. Here on the island, he was far more laid back. Less about controlling their activities as he was being a partner and teaching her things no one else had. This Michael was nicer, more reasonable. She watched him stand and view the slip of coast in sight below with his binoculars. His long legs had clambered easily over the more difficult parts of the trail. His trim torso was taut. "How are you so athletic?"

He lowered the binoculars. "I go mountain biking every week I can. There are four of us. We meet up and go together." He sat down beside her on the rocky surface. "Do you know Mark Zutka at Jam Bakery?"

She looked up, surprised. "Yeah. Is he one of the four?"

Michael nodded. "The other two are Fulton River cops: Issac Young and Patrick Doyle. We vary our trails, some are easier than others. Mark and Issac like the tougher ones. Patrick and I try to keep up."

All that biking explained Michael's muscular legs. She eyed him again as he stuffed his water bottle into his day pack. He was nice to look at. Good figure and, she had to admit, a great kisser. The memory of that wedding kiss hadn't left her. He would certainly be a top contender if she were looking for a guy to have a relationship with. *What am I thinking? If he knew what happened, he'd reject me outright.*

"Let's move on," Caroline said, getting to her feet.

They hiked a little farther, coming to a set of iron ladders and rungs to help them scramble up the mountain face. As these became more frequent and the slope more vertical, Caroline's can-do attitude started to wane. On the second half of the climbing section to a small ledge, there were ladders that required reaching beyond the ladder for widely spaced rungs. Michael went first, frequently turning back and holding out his hand to assist her, but she still refused his help. Until they reached the metal span that bridged a chasm between two sections of the trail.

Michael deftly walked across the span, his feet nimble on the metal, his hand holding a thin metal bar. He turned and held out his hand.

Caroline stood frozen at the start of the span. The bar was so slight. It didn't seem enough to hold on to as she crossed. The chasm was only ten feet wide, but if one fell, there was nothing to stop them from falling to their death. She shook her head in time with her trembling knees. "I can't," she called to Michael and backed away from the span.

"Yes, you can. You have to come across." He held out his hand to her as he stepped back on the span. "You can do this. Trust yourself. Trust your balance."

QUEST FOR LOVE

"I'll just return the way we came." She started to turn, but a line of people waited behind her.

"You can't go backward. You have to move forward. Have faith in yourself." He stepped a little closer to her side of the span. "Have faith in me."

She stared at him, her face filled with fear.

"Come on. Give me your hand." Michael waved his hand at her.

The people behind her were getting impatient. Calls of "come on, lady" and "You can do it" echoed behind her.

She reached out, her fingers not reaching Michael's.

"Another few inches. Come on, you're doing great," he coaxed her.

She slid her feet forward inches at a time. She grasped Michael's hand, squeezing hard, praying he didn't slip off the narrow beams and take her plummeting with him.

"Good grip. Come closer. That's it," he encouraged as she inched her way toward him while he stepped backward. When she glanced down and wobbled, her heart stopped. He called out. "Don't look down. Look at me."

Her eyes riveted on his as she slowly moved along, clutching the bar. A person behind Michael helped to guide him onto solid land. He didn't break eye contact with Caroline. "You're almost done."

As soon as Caroline's foot hit land, Michael pulled her forward, wrapped his arms around her, and hugged her tightly. She clung to him, her face buried in his neck.

The gathered crowd cheered and clapped at her accomplishment. They had to move out of the way as the waiting hikers stepped deftly across the beams and continued on the trail.

When she came to her senses again, and her racing heart returned to a normal rhythm, she stepped away from him. They sat down on a large boulder away from the chasm. "Thank you," she said, her eyes locking on to his.

"Of course. Thank *you* for trusting me."

His words sent a warm rush through her chest. It would be nice to have someone she could trust entirely. So far, he'd been nothing but helpful and trustworthy. If she could stop her automatic evasive reactions, perhaps they might have a good friendship.

The rest of the afternoon, Michael was solicitous of her needs. Pausing to let her rest when she knew perfectly well by just looking at him that he didn't need the pause. He was watching, protecting her as no one other than her brother ever had. While she had told him he didn't have to, she was grateful and a little tickled Michael was doing it.

That evening, they picked up a pizza and brought it back to the house. The cat was waiting for them on the kitchen stoop. Michael opened a can of tuna and placed half of it on the plate. Ringo devoured it. Then, he settled himself on the sofa for a snooze.

While at the pizza place, they heard the bridge replacement, a Bailey bridge like those used in World War II, was supposed to be opening tomorrow afternoon. The connection to the mainland would soon be restored.

"It's going to be crowded with all the people anxious to leave. I heard a lot of tourists were stuck here longer than they expected. We might have to wait for days in line to get across." Michael said, slipping another slice of veggie pizza on his plate.

"I have the house another week. Why not stay longer?" Caroline gnawed on the slice. The thought of Michael leaving, of being alone, made her uncomfortable. What if she had more nightmares? How would she fill her days? Who would she talk to?

"I've given up a week of business already. It's a darn good thing Gabriella was willing to return immediately and hold down the fort. I offered her a two thousand dollar bonus to entice her to come back. Besides, we need to find out if the money has been transferred into your account."

"Can't you call the bank or the trust fund manager?"

Michael raised his eyebrows at her. "And how would that look? I don't want to raise any suspicions." He paused, "Besides, my cell phone isn't working here. No cell signal."

Caroline stopped chewing. "The money might be there?" For some reason she couldn't understand, she didn't want this isolation, this simple living to end. There were a lot less complications without money. Her itch to spend money had diminished while they window-shopped around the island.

"It might be. Then, I can collect my share according to the pre-nup, and you can go on with your life. No job needed." Michael wiped his hands on a napkin.

She finished her slice. "You know, I wasn't very keen on the idea, but I enjoyed learning at Jam Bakery. It was nice to work with other people as a team." She pressed her napkin to her lips. "Have you heard of the Fulton River Women's Business Alliance?"

"Sure. They're quite an active group. They've managed to get more done to increase the tourism in two years than the men's Downtown Merchants Association has done in ten years."

"I went to one of their meetings and was amazed at all the female business workers and owners in town. It kinda sparked a wish to be one of them. Maybe own my own business someday."

His face brightened in surprise. "That's quite an endeavor. You have the money now to do it. Buy something already set up, or start your own."

"Yes, that's true. But I think I need more experience working."

Michael had raised his beer bottle to his mouth. He stopped at her words. "Are you going to keep working at Jam Bakery?"

She shrugged. "I'm not sure if it will be there, but there are other opportunities in Fulton River, or so I've been told."

"Like what?"

"Do you know Elowen Sparkle? She owns Sparkle Jewelry. She's looking for sales help." She winked at him. "And I know lots of things about jewelry and gems."

He sat back in his chair. "Sounds like a perfect match."

They went to bed early, Michael tucked away in his upstairs bedroom with the cat, who decided he wanted to remain inside for the night. Caroline retreated to her own bedroom on the first floor. Sleep came easier to her after the day's exertions. But her unwelcome visitor invaded her dreams.

Once again, she tried to fight him off, screaming, kicking, reaching for his eye sockets. His mass overwhelmed her; this time, her mother didn't open the library door. Did not stop the attack in progress; did not scream for Caroline's father to get this man out of the house. Someone called her name over and over again as she fell to the library's floor.

Her eyes popped open when her body hit the carpet. A figure beside her tried to help her up, but she shoved him away, and he retreated. The overhead light flicked on to reveal Michael standing against the wall, his eyes filled with concern. His brow furrowed, and his hands clasped together before his mouth tapping on his lips.

She sat up and burst into tears.

"Are you alright?" he asked. "Can I come closer?"

Her nod brought him to within a foot of her, on his knees beside her. "Can I help you up?" He held out his hand as he had done on the Beehive trail.

Without hesitation, she took it. She slumped down on the edge of the bed, but she didn't let go of his hand.

"Can I get you anything? Water?" He knelt before her, his thumb gently rubbing the back of her hand.

Tears erupted again. Her eyes pleaded with his. "Hold me."

He sat on the bed, wrapped his arms around her, and held on tight. "Nothing's going to harm you. I'll hold you as long as you want."

CHAPTER THIRTY-FIVE

Michael awoke in Caroline's bed, his arms around her as she slept. Her baby-fine blonde hair had escaped its braid and wound in his fingers like spun sunshine. Her eyes were closed, their light lashes thick and matted from tears. He wanted to get up, but he didn't dare move. Surprising her and having her flee was the last thing he wanted now that he had her in his arms.

Sunlight streamed through the window, hitting them both with its rays. She stirred, turned her face toward his torso, and rubbed her nose against his bare chest. It tickled, and he tried not to chuckle but couldn't help it. The little noise he made was enough to bring her awake. She arched her head back until her terror-filled eyes met his. Seeing him, they softened.

"Good morning," he said, still unmoving. Her eyes were bloodshot and surrounded by dark circles. If she retreated, that was her prerogative. He wasn't going to make her.

To his surprise, she didn't. "I had another bad dream last night."

He nodded. "You asked me to hold you."

"Hmm." She rolled onto her back away from him.

He remained on his side, facing her. "Would you like to talk about it?"

Caroline was quiet. "I'm not sure I can," she whispered.

"Someone hurt you. I understand that much, and I don't need to know anymore. Except if there's something I can do to help you deal with the PTSD, please let me know."

Tears silently rolled out of the corners of her eyes, dripping onto the bed sheet. "It was a long time ago. I was—" She stopped. "My mother walked in on it and interceded. My parents argued about whether they should call the police or hide the incident. They decided it was better for my father—and me—to do the latter. It was kept hushed because of my father's status as a US senator."

Michael was sure he could hear her heart pounding. "Was he ever arrested?"

"Oh no. That would make the papers." Her voice dripped with sarcasm. "He was fired and told to get the hell out of Vermont."

"And you?" Michael had a feeling he already knew the answer. "Did you get any ... uh, help?"

"No. I was shipped off to Switzerland for boarding and finishing school." Her tears slowed. "I think they thought removing me from the scene of the assault would be enough for me to pretend it never happened." She shrugged. "It didn't work, of course. The mind doesn't let go of such traumatic things easily, if ever." She leaned into him for a second before she seemed to realize it and pulled away again. "It at least got me out from under their constant supervision and harping. I was happy to be away someplace where I could control *their* access to me, too."

Michael wiped the nearest course of tears off her cheek with his index finger. "Should I get up and leave you? Or do you need another hug?"

She bobbed her head. "I need some time alone."

He got up. At the door, he turned back. "Coffee?" He shut the door behind him when she shook her head. He didn't want to push. He understood enough.

Back in his room, he ruminated over everything. A flashback to the UMass party kept replaying in his brain. He'd meant to talk with her, but as he approached, another guy got to her side first, and she'd given him her full attention. He'd backed off but kept his eye on her, hoping to renew the effort if the guy left. But something else happened. The guy slung his arm around her shoulders and hugged her to him. Caroline's reaction had been swift. Her whole body tensed. She flung off his arm, gave the guy a glare, and stalked out of the room. He never saw her return. She hadn't been any more interested in intimacy even back then.

Her description of what happened, of being sent to boarding and finishing school in Switzerland, suggested it happened while she was young, perhaps in her pre-teen years.

He didn't want to think about the possibilities. They were too appalling to consider.

Caroline remained in bed. She remembered asking Michael to hold her. She'd been out of her mind, suffering the lingering effects of the nightmare. Clearly, she would never have asked him to do that if she were in her right mind. And yet, there had been some trust building between them. He was easy to talk with, and he didn't push. His friendship and concern were chipping away at the walls she'd built around her after the incident. So much so the feeling of this man's arms around her made her feel safe and secure instead of vulnerable and afraid.

The thought that Michael could seep into her confidence was unsettling and yet not surprising. She knew he meant it when he said he was only trying to help her: help her stay solvent, out of bankruptcy, out of the news and tabloid press. So far, he'd been true to his word. She was determined to mull over the incident and her scrambled feelings for this guy who was now her husband. And if him breaking through that wall held true, it most certainly was an emotional breakthrough for her.

An hour later, he entered the kitchen to make breakfast, relieved to find Caroline already there. A mug was in her hand, and a pot of coffee was still hot in the coffeemaker. The cat sat basking in a ray of sunshine streaming through the window.

"Well, are you taking over breakfast this morning?" Michael poured himself a full mug and sat at the table across from her.

"Not only no, but hell no. You cook far better food than I do." She sipped at her mug. "I was kinda hoping you'd cook up more bacon. We have some tomatoes and lettuce." She sat back in her chair and smiled. "I think I'd like a BLT for breakfast. And I think your cat would like some bacon, too."

"He is a hungry kitty." Michael grinned down at the cat. "A BLT sounds delicious. You got it." He started to rise from the table, but she stopped him.

"Wait. I want to talk with you first." She watched as he settled back in his seat. "Are you still planning on leaving today?"

He set his mug down. He wanted to stay. And she seemed to want him to as well. But he needed to get some things straightened out as soon as possible. "I really need to get back to the office."

She glowered at him. "So you've done your duty, and now you're going to run?"

"No, no. It's not like that. I have a lot of financial things hanging of my own, plus there's my family. I told my mother and Alan I was leaving on vacation but left no other information. They might have been trying to contact me about something. Without cell service here, they might not have gotten through."

"Like what?" she demanded, setting her mug down hard on the table surface.

He shrugged, "It could be a client who has an immediate problem, or there's been a sickness or accident in my family."

"What about me? I am your wife now. Don't I figure into your plans?"

His head spun like a yo-yo. *All of a sudden, she's pulling the marriage card?* "Caroline, really. You know this marriage is in name only, and it's temporary. You made sure of that in the prenup."

"Still, I would think you'd stay with me a little longer. Besides, I haven't authorized the money transfer yet."

Michael's heart stopped. "We have an agreement."

QUEST FOR LOVE

"Yes, you needed my money!"

"And you needed my help getting it! But you didn't want a real husband. You wanted some rollover who would take the money and leave. Someone you could trust to sign a prenup with a no-intimacy clause." Frustration and fury building inside him, he added, "What's wrong with intimacy? Or did you pick me because you thought I wouldn't balk?" He started pacing the kitchen, aware she watched his every move. "Did you think I was never attracted to you? That I had no desire for intimacy with you? That I wouldn't want a future that might involve you and me together? Well, you were wrong."

He glared at her expression of surprise. Hadn't she known or figured it out? He scrubbed his face with his palm. "I've wanted to get to know you since I first saw you in my father's office. I even tried coming on to you at the UMass party years ago. I have never stopped wanting to explore a relationship with you. But here we are. In a phony marriage. I'm honored you chose me. And as hard as it's been, I've honored your damn no-intimacy clause. You owe me that money!"

His pronouncement took her breath away. He'd played cool, even cold, and all that time, he'd wanted to have a relationship with her. For her money. Just like every other man she'd ever met. "Fine. Take your money. Just wait a few months before you file for divorce."

An hour later, a cab waited for Michael in the driveway. He picked up his duffle bag and climbed in without looking backward. Without saying goodbye.

She watched from the kitchen window as the cab pulled away, then padded back to her room, the cat following her like a shadow. She'd had no idea Michael thought that way about her. Looking back on the past three weeks, she had never detected a single clue of his attraction to her. Even that night at the UMass party. He had tried to pick her up, but so did every other guy there. Michael was just as handsome back then as he was now. She had seen him approaching when another guy interrupted. She'd decided it was for the best. To keep Michael at a distance, she moved on to the newest guy vying for her attention. But her eyes followed him around the room, watching him chat up a couple of girls before disappearing into another room.

Ringo nudged at her hand, asking to be petted. Caroline absentmindedly complied as she stared out the window at the ocean view. There were quite a few sailboats out on the water. She reached for the binoculars to check out a schooner as it came into view. The binoculars were gone. In their place was an envelope with a one hundred dollar bill and a note.

> "I know there's a lot of food still left in the house, but I wanted to leave you with this in case something comes up or some shiny bauble catches your fancy. Your h., Michael."

"Your h," she repeated. "Husband?" The idea of Michael as a real husband filled Caroline's core with warmth. He would make a great husband. *And with a body like that...ugh, don't think about it. He'd probably make a great lover too.* Well, it was out of the question now. He'd expressed his disdain for her lifestyle, her dependence on money, and her fake friends. She knew he was right. Her beauty might be only skin deep, but vanity saturated her being.

Could he ever love me? If I made some changes? Dump the friends who had already dumped me? Control my spending to a more normal level?

A wave of sadness filled her heart. *It might be too late.*

CHAPTER THIRTY-SIX

Caroline spent her day poking in Somesville with the crisp one hundred dollar bill deep in her jeans pocket. The downtown sparkled like the quaint, New England small town it was. As it was getting closer to Memorial Day, the crowds had increased. With the bridge open again, even more would invade the tiny island. Window-shopping, she decided, was a cheap thrill. And if she found something that struck her fancy, she could buy it. The thought buoyed her spirits.

During her first window-shopping experience with Michael, she had tried to make a mental list of all the things she wanted to come back to buy when her trust money was dispersed. Now, she looked at the bright, shiny things, thought how cute or functional this or that was, and moved on to the next window. The thought came to her that half the stuff she had in storage was like that. Cute and non-functional. Only taking up space and collecting dust.

Her eyes were clearer. They could see the trinkets and stuff she filled her life with were not filling the need she had. The need to be loved, appreciated, and respected. It didn't take money, designer clothes, or fancy cars. What she needed and what she wanted instead was someone to love her and someone she could love. With tears in her eyes, she realized she'd found that man and lost him again in less than a week. A tug of deep longing filled her from the crown of her head to the tips of her self-pedicured toes.

She returned to the house, the one hundred dollar bill still nestled in her pocket. Her hopes swung high that Michael had returned. Maybe he couldn't get across the temporary bridge. Maybe he was still waiting in line to cross. Her insides deflated when she realized he wasn't there. *Of course, he wasn't in the house. He left his key on the kitchen table.* The thought gave her hope he might still return, knocking on the door for her to let him in.

Should I? She pondered the question, looking out on the ocean far below the house. The flutter in her chest answered for her. She *would* let him in. She missed him and all his self-sufficient ways. He could teach her so much. She blinked back the flood of tears. These last three weeks had made her feel like she should and could take care of herself. She should take charge of her life and make something of it instead of frittering her time away. Even her time at the Women's Business Alliance had made her feel like she should start her own business—to seek her own destiny. Seeing so many happy, successful women made her want to be part of *their* crowd.

In the past few days, Michael had made her feel like she could change her life, turn it around, and make good use of it.

A tear spilled down her cheek. She brushed it away. She hadn't prayed in a very long time, but now she found herself praying Michael would return.

She microwaved a couple slices of leftover pizza for dinner and poured herself a generous glass of wine. Curled up on the couch with Ringo snoozing beside her, she tried to finish reading the book she had brought.

Her thoughts kept veering to Michael. Where was he? Why hadn't he returned? He made it sound like he loved her. He'd all but said the words. Just the thought of what he said made her heart sing. The funny sensation made her feel giddy. A giggle burst from her lips, and then she became tense and silent. "I love him." She didn't know where that had come from, but she was dead sure it was true. She loved him, she trusted him, and she wanted him to come back. Picking up her cell phone, she clicked it on to dial. But as usual, there wasn't any connection. With a heavy sigh, she returned to her book after saying yet another prayer that he would return.

Frustrated with the entire situation, she retired to her bed with Ringo snuggled up beside her. She stroked his soft fur and listened to him purring happily. The sound gave her comfort. He enjoyed being with her and, to tell the truth, so did she. He licked her hand, bringing tears to her eyes. The cat's compassion was nothing like being held by Michael, but it warmed her heart. It occurred to her she had minimal physical contact in her life. Before Michael, the only persons who touched her regularly besides her brother and his wife were a paid masseuse and an esthetician. This expression of care bolstered her spirits but also made her wish harder for Michael to return.

There was a hearty knocking on the kitchen door. "Michael!" The cat bolted out of the bedroom. Caroline jumped out of bed and ran for the door barefoot and without her robe. The cool night air hit her squarely in the chest when she yanked open the door.

"Well, hello, Caroline."

Leaning against the door jamb was Donald. His face filled with delight as his eyes devoured her silky nightgown.

Caroline screamed and tried to slam the door, but his palm caught it and shoved it back. He strode toward her triumphantly.

She turned and ran, her eyes frantically searching for something, anything that could be a weapon. The fire poker. She snatched it up and turned. Donald wasn't there. Where had he gone?

A sound in the kitchen made her swing around. Donald stood, a chef's knife in one hand, Ringo squirming in the other. "Come here, or I'll carve up your cat like a Thanksgiving turkey."

Caroline's knees weakened further at the thought of that maniac harming Ringo. Maybe if she played it cool, he'd leave Ringo alone. "That's not my cat."

The poker was far longer than the knife, but he could throw the knife. She could not throw the poker.

"Doesn't matter." His leer broadened. "Look at you." He licked his lips. "An image of supreme loveliness. I've never stopped thinking about you and our short time together. Then I realized we can have so much more fun now that you're all grown up." He took a step forward, ignoring Ringo's loud protests. "I didn't appreciate it when your momma came to the rescue. And your father fired me. Fired. Can you imagine my distress? And then you left me all alone at Chez d'Avignon. I was so looking forward to talking with you. Catching up on the things we've done in that absence." His gaze raked over her. "Show me what you've learned."

Caroline's knees trembled at his words. He was going to rape her. Perhaps kill her with that knife so she couldn't talk. *Talk. I must keep him talking. Maybe it will stall his actions.* "We can talk now. How did you find me?"

"That was the easy part. I knocked on your townhouse door, but someone else answered. He told me you sold it to him. It didn't take long to check the internet to find out that was true. But I couldn't find your new address. Google found your profile on the Single & Free website during that online inquiry. It surprised me to see your profile and picture. It was a sign." His eyes glittered. "You gave me an opening. It was time to put my plans into action."

"But how did you find me here? I didn't tell anyone but Tony where I was going."

He took another step into the living room. "It was easy. Do you remember I wasn't seated at the table when you arrived at the restaurant?" When she nodded, he continued. "That's because I was outside on the street. I attached a GPS tracking tag to your car where you would never, ever see it. The map showed me everywhere you went." He smirked at her. "Did you enjoy the inn in Haston?"

Caroline's heart stopped.

"Don't worry. I wasn't anywhere near you then." He held up his index finger. "Though I sorely wanted to spring my surprise on you there. There were too many people around." He held up the knife again and ran his thumb across the sharp edge. "Too many people who might hear you screaming."

QUEST FOR LOVE

Fear clutching her body, she tightened her grip on the poker. "I have a friend. He's coming back. Tonight." She had to say something to make Donald leave, to put off his intentions.

"We better get to it then." He smiled crazily, his eyes staring but unfocused. "We have to have another go. We just have to." He stepped closer.

"Put down the cat and the knife, and I'll cooperate."

He eyed her suspiciously. "I'm not sure I believe you." He motioned his head toward the poker in her hand.

Caroline slowly placed the poker on the table.

Donald stepped closer, the menacing knife still in his hand, Ringo still squirming, tucked against his side.

When he was within reach, she acted. She snatched up the poker and smashed Donald in the head with all the force she could muster. It didn't pull free. In sickening horror, Caroline realized the pointed end of the poker had penetrated his skull. Ringo flew from Donald's arm and scurried away.

Donald stumbled forward, a weird expression on his face. He pulled the poker out of his head. Blood erupted, running down the slide and back of his head. He stumbled forward, reaching out to grab her.

Caroline evaded his reach. There was movement behind him in the kitchen. Michael slammed the heavy cast iron frying pan to the other side of Donald's head. Donald dropped to the floor, unmoving.

"Get to your car," Michael shouted. When she didn't move, he yelled, "NOW!"

"The cat," she yelled, reaching for it under the coffee table.

"I'll get him. Get out of the house."

She grabbed her keys off the sofa table and fled out the front door. Her car sat where she had left it. The GPS. Where had he placed it? Would he follow her using it?

Michael exited the house, heading toward her with Ringo tucked under his arm.

"Is he alive?" Her voice trembled as she spoke. She prayed he wasn't. She didn't ever want to deal with him again. She prayed he was dead with all her might.

"He fell on the knife when he hit the ground." He wrapped his free arm around her and pulled her close. "He's dead."

Caroline willingly gave up her car keys in exchange for Ringo's furry warmth. They drove to the nearest open business, a gas station, and called the police. After Michael briefly explained what happened, the police called backup, and all of them returned to the house. Caroline clung to Michael's hand outside on the lawn while the police went inside.

"What will they do?"

Michael wrapped his arms around her and held her close. "I expect they'll take us to the police station for questioning. Separately, no doubt."

His prediction was spot on. After more police arrived, a female officer escorted her to one cruiser while a male officer placed Michael in another. Ringo was returned to the house and shut into a bathroom to stay out of the crime scene area.

The two vehicles were far enough apart to prohibit talking if they managed to open the windows. But close enough, they could see each other. Michael waved and gave her a thumbs-up. She dissolved into tears before his eyes, her sobs escalating, but he was helpless to do anything but watch in frustration.

Within the hour, they were at the police station for interrogation. Michael had hoped they would bring Donald's body out in a body bag so Caroline could see he was dead. It might help her, might relieve some of her nightmares. His interrogation wasn't bad. They had listened to his entire explanation and asked a few questions, then let him go. He waited in the police station for Caroline. She was going to need him when they were through with her.

Caroline cried throughout her questioning. She told them her father was a senator for Vermont, probably in Washington DC for the upcoming Memorial Day festivities. She also made it clear she didn't want him notified or the press to catch wind of the incident if at all possible. While they couldn't promise anything, they said they'd do what they could to protect her identity. Especially after hearing the entire story from the afternoon in the library to the date at Chez d'Avignon, stalking her to her townhouse and then to the island. She mentioned that he had placed a GPS device in or on her car. The detective said they would check for the device. She waited patiently, drained but unable to shut her eyes and rest. The police searched her vehicle and found the device, confirming her story.

 She walked into Michael's open arms four hours later as the eastern sky lightened. The motors of fishing boats were clear on the calm waters of the bay. "I don't ever want to go back to that house," she whispered in a shuddering voice. Knowing the house was locked down as a crime scene, Michael had found them a hotel room with the help of the police. He also arranged for someone to feed Ringo at the house.

 It felt like another nightmare. She was numb. Too tired and too numb to sleep. Michael lay beside her on the bed, his arms warm and strong around her.

 "Why did you come back?" Caroline asked, her voice barely audible. She could feel Michael's arm tighten around her.

 His voice was soft, his lips against her ear. "I got all the way home. Sat in the driveway and stared at the house. And I realized that's not where I wanted to be. Where I needed to be." He paused before adding, "You need me, and I need you." He paused again, adding with a tremor,

"Because I realized I love you whether or not you feel the same about me."

He loved her. She wasn't sure exactly how she felt about him. Grateful he had arrived just when he did, thankful she hadn't had to face the investigation alone, and relieved he had stepped up and taken care of their needs. Caroline considered herself competent in managing her affairs, but this entire situation, from the dress to today, had overwhelmed her.

When she didn't respond to his declaration, he said, "Close your eyes. You're safe."

She fell asleep to Michael's warm lips pressing a kiss on her forehead.

During the night, Caroline stirred while deep in the grasp of another nightmare. Michael soothed her brow, bringing her back to consciousness and repeating, "He's dead. He can't hurt you anymore." Caroline clung to him as he held her. The image of Donald, the crazed look in his eyes, faded as Michael's arms tightened. He started gently rocking their bodies, spooned together on the king-sized bed. She fell back to a quiet sleep.

When her breathing slowed and steadied, Michael thought of his declaration and her failure to respond in any way. So she didn't feel as he did. Didn't love him and couldn't acknowledge she needed him. Considering all she had gone through in the last fourteen hours, he shouldn't be surprised. There were a lot of emotions for her to process. He'd wait. With his fingers crossed, he'd wait as long as it took for her to figure out how she felt about him. He closed his eyes and let sleep overtake him.

He kept her active for the next two days. Bar Harbor's downtown kept Caroline's mind occupied as there were so many shops. They walked up the road to the top of Cadillac Mountain, where they had a picnic of bottled water, fruit, and sandwiches purchased that morning. The view of all the surrounding islands off the coast gave him the idea to book them a boat tour if they weren't allowed to leave the island later that day.

Dinner was at the Terrace Restaurant, where they could enjoy the light breezes under a blanket of stars. The reflection of distant lights across Frenchman's Bay twinkled on the water. A cruise ship was anchored not far off and its passengers would disembark in the morning. *Good thing we'll be out of downtown.*

"Do you think we'll be free to leave tomorrow?" Caroline asked between sips of wine.

Michael relaxed back in his chair. "I hope not. I've booked us for the lighthouse and puffin cruise tomorrow morning. I hope you don't get seasick."

"That sounds good. I don't get seasick. Or at least I didn't when I traveled across the Mediterranean from Monte Carlo to Greece."

He suddenly worried his attempt at entertaining her might not be enough. Enough to keep her from reliving the horror. "Okay, then. We'll take the cruise after breakfast. The guide said we might even see whales while we're out."

Her eyes brightened at the word "whales," and his pulse quickened, knowing his plan had scored. For a moment, he debated asking the question that had been bugging him for weeks. The answer was necessary to his own understanding of the entire situation. "There's something that's been bothering me. I just don't understand why you agreed to marry David Wescott Hayes in the first place. You said you didn't love him."

Her smile disappeared, and her face went pale. She looked away as if gathering her thoughts then explained, "My mother introduced me to David. She kept telling me that with my father's political connections and his father's domestic and international business connections, it was the perfect match for our elite social stratum. She kept drilling into me that it would be the society wedding of the decade."

Caroline shrugged. "I don't know. I guess I got tired of her pushing. So when David proposed, I said yes to get them both off my back." She rolled her eyes, "Which, of course, led to even more issues at the wedding. My mother wanted it to be the wedding to top all. By the time the day rolled around, I was sick to death of the entire farce. My gut kept telling me David wasn't in love with me, that he had to be in it for the money he knew I would collect after the wedding occurred."

Michael's mind churned with the story. It made sense. "You and David, you never..."

Caroline shook her head. "No. I made him agree to wait until our wedding night. I think he thought I was still a virgin and he was happy enough to wait." She clasped her hands together. "He wasn't after my body anyway, so it didn't matter to him." She gave him a single-shoulder shrug.

They both stared out into the moonlit waters of Frenchmen's Bay.

"There's something else I should tell you," Caroline whispered. "But not here. Someone might overhear."

"Let's go for a walk and find a secluded space when we leave here."

After dinner, they strolled the downtown streets again. The tourist traffic was still light. For such a beautiful evening, Michael would have expected more pedestrians. As they paused alone on the ocean walk to look out at the darkened silhouettes of the Porcupine islands, Caroline took his hand. "You need to know about Randy."

Michael gestured her toward a park bench. It was secluded under a pine tree far from the nearest pathways or sidewalks. They sat down.

Caroline inhaled, held her breath for several seconds, and then exhaled. "Randy was my first boyfriend. I was in college in Northampton at the time. We met at a bar. He was charismatic, very friendly, had a great sense of humor, and sought out fun everywhere he went. I fell in love with him pretty fast and hard." She paused and exhaled sharply.

"Go on," Michael said, taking her hand.

"At first, he was affectionate and loving. We started an intimate relationship. It was pleasing in the beginning. As time went on, he started to change." She looked up at the few stars visible despite the full moon. "He started demanding I follow his rules. In essence, he became controlling. If I didn't do what he asked, or talked to another man, or even went out with friends without him, he'd assault me. My brother noticed the bruises. Then, suddenly, Randy left. I found out just recently that my father bribed him to leave me."

Her eyes glazed as she spoke. "About the time I was getting ready to marry David, Randy came back. He apologized, said he'd changed. I felt that tug of attraction as before. We started up a relationship again." She looked him in the eyes. "But just like before, the rules and the abuse started. Long story, but suffice to say, he was after my money, too. He kidnapped me and made a run for the Canadian border, thinking my passport and father's senatorial seat could get him over the border. It was there he was apprehended by border police for outstanding warrants for armed robberies. That was the last I've seen of Randy."

Michael's mind raced with the essential facts. She'd had a lover. She wasn't afraid of having a sexual relationship itself. Only that the previous relationship had turned violent. Violent, as had the incident with Donald.

Caroline inhaled deeply again and exhaled slowly. "Thank you for everything you've done to protect me. It's been horrific these past three days. I'm so grateful you were with me." She sniffled and brushed her cheek. "You saved me."

Michael brushed away the tears spilling down her cheeks. "I'm grateful I was able to protect you. Thankful I came back when I did." He remembered the gut feeling that he needed to go back. It was the kind of strong feeling he never failed to listen to. Listening to it had saved him countless times. This time, it saved the person he loved.

"I'm sorry I'm such a stubborn, spoiled, incompetent woman." Her tear-filled eyes bore into his. The lashes were wet with tears, her cheeks flushed from the wine.

He brushed aside a stray lock of hair from her face. "No. Don't think of yourself that way. You cannot help how you were raised. Your parents might have meant well, but failing to teach you some of the basics of living was unfathomable. It's not your fault."

Caroline huffed. "Maybe it isn't. But now I have so much to learn. Like how to write a check. I've never used one because I don't know how."

"My father did it for you. I'd be happy to give you a lesson," Michael offered, wrapping his arm around her shoulders as they walked back to their hotel.

"Hmm. Maybe when we get back."

Michael laughed. "It will have to wait until we get back. I don't have one with me."

"Another thought I had was to take a small sum of money, and place it into a checking account I can manage on my own."

"That's a great idea. I can set that up for you back in Vermont."

She squeezed his hand. "No. That's another thing I'd like to do on my own. It's time I learned how to do things myself."

They returned from the puffin cruise the next afternoon and were eating lunch on the deck at the Cuban restaurant when the detective called. "You're free to leave the island. We have all the information and evidence we need. The house has been cleaned up, so you can return anytime. Just stop by the police station for the key," the voice on the speaker said.

Michael disconnected the call. "Well, do you want to go today or wait until tomorrow?"

QUEST FOR LOVE

Caroline's cheeks were pale, her lips pressed tightly together. "I don't want to go but need my things." Her eyes implored Michael.

"I can go in if you want to stay in the car—"

Thinking better of it, she cut off his offer. "I think I need to go in. It might help close this horrid chapter."

Michael squeezed her hand. "Sure. Let's go in the morning,"

They collected Caroline's belongings from the house. Michael went with her, his arm about her shoulder as they walked through the kitchen and living room, past where Donald had fallen. Whatever mess had been there was cleaned up. Ringo came out from the bathroom to greet them as soon as the door was opened. Caroline stopped to give him a pat as she hastily stuffed her things into her suitcases. He rubbed against her legs, seemingly grateful for saving him. Michael gathered their food from the kitchen into grocery bags. All except a can of cat food.

"His last meal?" Caroline said, hefting her suitcase beside the kitchen door.

"One for the road." Michael fed him before taking him out to the Mustang in a carrier he'd purchased.

"You're bringing him home?" Caroline asked.

"Sure. Perhaps my mother and her rescue group can find him a good home." Michael said as he settled the carrier behind the driver's seat and went back inside. "I'm not going to leave the little guy alone to fend for himself."

"Why can't you keep him?" She grabbed two grocery bags and followed Michael lugging her suitcases.

As they packed the tiny Mustang fastback's rear seat to the hilt, he said, "I live at my Mom's house, as do four foster cats. I'm not sure Ringo would be welcome, but Mom can find him a new home."

Caroline was silent as she buckled herself into the front passenger seat. "I'll take him."

Michael stared at her. "Are you sure? Is Tony going to allow pets?"

"He will for me."

Michael steered the car down the drive, glancing once to make sure they hadn't left anything behind. Seeing nothing, he sped up, noticing Caroline's gaze was firmly ahead. "Do you mind if we stop someplace? I don't want the last thing we remember of this island to be this house."

"Whatever you want," she replied.

They stopped at Otter Cove, taking one last look at the Atlantic from the safety of the large granite slabs along the shoreline. The retreating tide had left behind a water puddle in a shallow basin-like indent in the rocky surface. As they watched quietly, a seagull splashed in the puddle, ruffling its feathers as though bathing. Side by side, leaning against each other's shoulders, they enjoyed the quiet, peacefulness of the scene. Satisfied with the tranquility of their time there, they gathered themselves back into the Mustang, and Michael drove all three of them home.

CHAPTER THIRTY-SEVEN

Michael had a lot of explaining to do when he got home. First to his mother, then his siblings. He told them everything except about getting married and Donald's home invasion. It was best not to add more mouths that could become loose lips.

Back at the office, he found Gabriella pleased to see him, even if it was only four days later than he'd said he'd be back. Her ire was short-lived when Michael held out the promised money in cash.

His office time was spent investing the bulk of Caroline's money in sound stocks, paying off her bill and tying up all kinds of miscellaneous loose threads. The trust executor did call to inquire about a rumor that he and Caroline were married but living apart.

"Seriously, I admit we are, temporarily. Caroline's living in her brother's tiny condo right now. I've been overwhelmed with work since we returned. So much so I haven't had time to even think about moving my things there."

"I know how it is. Took me three months before I moved the last of my things to our new home when I got married. I think you'll be a stabilizing help for her." The executor clicked his tongue. "Between you and me, I've been sweating over this issue. Repeatedly, I've searched for loopholes just in case she married some scumbag. I'm relieved she chose wisely for a change. Congratulations."

When the man hung up, Michael gave a hearty sigh of relief. The executor was pleased to hear he and Caroline had married. There was no need to try to look the part of a happy married, in love couple when they clearly weren't at all.

They met for dinner at Bailey's Tavern a few days after returning to Fulton River. The restaurant was nearly empty when they arrived. She looked nervous but restless, and Michael waited while she screwed up her courage to say whatever it was she wanted to discuss with him.

They talked about their first days back in town. Michael spent his first night home answering his family's questions about the trip. "I didn't mention the marriage or how things ended on the island. I didn't even mention you were there. Not knowing which way this was going to go." He thanked the waiter for the beer and watched him walk away before asking, "How was your homecoming?"

"Tony knew I was going away for a few weeks, but he didn't know about us. Jamaica also knew I was going away for a vacation. I told them it was lovely, and I managed to get some hiking and relaxation in. I didn't mention anything else."

Michael felt his chest cave. He was hoping she'd have decided what to do with their ruse of a marriage. It sounded like she hadn't yet. "Yeah, no sense."

"True." Caroline gave a curt nod. "I've been doing a lot of thinking."

His pulse rate kicked into high gear. Did he dare to hope? The look on her face, the tense jaw, her inability to look him in the eye. He knew what was coming. "Oh..."

"I would like you, as my accountant, to give me a cashier's check for ten thousand dollars from my investments."

Michael's eyebrows rose in unison. "Whatever for?"

"I want to open that checking account I talked about while we were ... uh, on the island."

He eyed her suspiciously. "I can do that for you. Make a direct transfer to a new account I can activate and—"

"No. As I explained earlier, I need to do this for myself. I don't want you to have access."

"You don't trust me?" Stunned, his voice rose an octave as he collapsed back in his chair.

Caroline took a quick inhale and a fast exhale. "Of course I trust you. I need to start acting like a responsible adult instead of a spoiled, useless brat who has to hire people to do what she should be doing for herself."

He studied her before replying. "Of course, as your accountant, I will get you that check, tomorrow if you'd like."

Caroline smiled and reached across the table to still Michael's hand on his beer bottle. "I have to learn how to handle money properly. Thank you for cooperating."

He gathered his courage and asked the million-dollar question. "What other changes are you making?"

"I'm staying at Tony's condo a little longer. I'll pay him back for the month of use and rent going forward."

"I'll give him a call to arrange payments," Michael said, his spirits buoyed to be able to do something to help her.

"Don't bother. I'll pay out of my new checking account," she said forcefully. "I also need to go through my storage units. I believe Salvation Army or Goodwill will be happy to assist me in purging my life of a truckload of unnecessary stuff."

"I can hel—" Michael started to say reflexively until he saw the hard glint in her eyes. "Okay," he sighed. "Do it yourself."

"I intend to," she said with a happy but smug expression.

"How are you going to cover your rent? Ten K isn't going to last long."

Caroline's smile lit up his sagging emotions. "I'm going to be working at Jam Bakery for a few more weeks. It's strawberry season coming up soon, so I'll help make more jams." She straightened in her chair. "And, I hope to join Elowen Sparkle's shop as a saleswoman. If she hasn't filled the position yet."

He tried to smile and look enthusiastic for her. She was getting on with her life. His insides ached for any indication she still wanted him. She hadn't said a word about how their marriage would play out. Would it be as planned in the prenuptial agreement? Or would she want to stay together with him? It wasn't looking good for the latter scenario.

"How's Ringo faring?" Michael asked to change the subject.

"He's doing great. He has the entire condo to himself. He treats *me* like a servant!" She started to giggle, "Now I know what it feels like."

Michael couldn't help but laugh.

Their dinners came, and their conversation dropped off.

Caroline could see the disappointment in his eyes and in the slump of his shoulders. She knew he wanted to help, but it was high time she got off her lazy arse and did things for herself.

At the end of the meal, she gathered that courage again and said, "I know you were hoping for some kind of resolution between us. I'm not ready for that yet."

He blinked several times, sitting stiffly in his chair, his hands clasped in his lap.

"I started psychotherapy again. It's helping to diminish my nightmares of Donald. It's also helped me realize the reason behind my attraction to Randy. In a few months, I hope to make decisions about my future life."

Michael glanced down at his hands before looking at her again. "Let me know when you decide. You know where I'll be."

Later that evening, she scrolled through the emails and text messages she couldn't read while on the island. At least half of them were from Rachel. Rather than read them all, she called her friend. "What's up, girl?"

"Where have you been? I've sent all kinds of messages," Rachel said with an angry tone of voice.

QUEST FOR LOVE

"I told you I was going away for a few weeks. What's so urgent?" Ringo climbed into her lap and settled down. "Make yourself at home, why don't you?" Caroline murmured.

"What? Who's there?" Rachel demanded. "Oh! Do you have company?" The suggestive lilt in her voice made Caroline cringe.

"No one but my new cat," she confessed.

"Y-you? You have a cat?" Rachel sputtered.

"Never mind. What's going on?"

"Merrick proposed! I'm so excited! His family wants us to marry at Thanksgiving so everyone can attend. And I pick you to be my maid of honor."

Rachel was getting married to a man she didn't love. For his money. She felt sorry for her friend, not having met someone she could love. *Like you love Michael.* It only took a moment for her to decide. "Thank you for the honor of your offer, but I can't do it."

"What?" Rachel screeched over the line. "You won't do it? Why not?"

Caroline's response was firm. "Doesn't matter. Pick someone else. I'm not even sure I'll attend."

"But you could meet so many rich guys looking for a beautiful wife," Rachel whined.

"Not interested." It was true. She didn't want to stand up for a couple getting married for convenience.

Her brain screeched to a halt. *Isn't that what you and Michael did?* The thought made her flush with embarrassment. They had made a marriage of convenience. But it wasn't meant to be a permanent one. Thanks to the prenup, they were able to walk away, get a divorce and live fulfilling lives elsewhere. "I have to go," she told Rachel and disconnected. The sourness in her belly kept her company all night.

The next day, Caroline went to Jam Bakery for breakfast. She could have made it herself after Michael's lessons, but she had yet to buy groceries. Her pocket held a grocery store list she'd need on the way home after this morning's breakfast.

Jamaica spotted her in line to order. "Caroline! You're back!" She gave Caroline a bear hug. "When are you coming back to work? I've a load of fresh strawberries arriving tomorrow. Want to help Isabelle make jam?"

Caroline shrugged one shoulder. "Sure. I'd love to. What time?"

They made arrangements and walked over to a table to wait for Caroline's order.

She gathered her courage and burst into the real reason she'd come in today. "Actually, I have a big favor to ask you."

Jamaica cocked her head. "I'm listening."

"I've never had to manage my money. Henry DuBois always did it for me. I'm hoping you could show me how to manage a checking account."

A broad smile spread across Jamaica's face. "I can do that, no problem. Do you have the account set up yet?"

"No, I'm heading there after leaving here."

Their conversation was interrupted by Elowen Sparkle. "Good morning, ladies. What's happening?" Today, her hair was dyed in rainbow colors, the prominent color, chartreuse, matched her poufy peasant skirt.

One of Jamaica's employees waved her back to the cash register. "Excuse me for a few minutes, ladies. I'll be right back."

Caroline knew this was her chance. She gave Elowen a bright smile. "I was going to stop by your store this afternoon if you're going to be there. Are you still looking for sales help?"

"I hired someone last week. Why? Were you interested in applying?"

"I am, or was. I know a lot about jewelry."

Elowen gave her a wink. "If this girl doesn't work out, I'll let you know." She cupped her hand around her mouth and whispered,

QUEST FOR LOVE

"Between you and me, she's not likely to last. Late every day this week so far, and it's her first week of work! I'll be happy to consider you for the job. In the meantime, stop by any time and see the shop."

Jamaica was heading back to the table. Elowen paused before adding, "There's a Women's Alliance meeting tonight if you'd like to go."

Jamaica rolled her eyes. "I was just going to tell her about that."

Elowen rubbed Jamaica's shoulder. "Doesn't matter as long as she says yes."

The two women stared at her, waiting for a response. A trickle of warmth filled her chest. They wanted her to attend. Could she count these women as real friends? It seemed like it. "I'd love to. As long as everything goes well at the bank."

Caroline continued at Elowen's puzzled look, "I'm opening an account. Jamaica's going to teach me how to handle it."

"Excellent choice in a teacher," Elowen said, her hand resting on Jamaica's shoulder again. "This woman is a force of nature and has it all figured out." She glanced over her shoulder as the saleswoman called out her order for pickup. "Ask the bank about their free money management course. I think it's coming up soon. I have to go. Great seeing you both. I'll see you tonight."

Caroline and Jamaica said their goodbyes to Elowen. As Caroline got up to get her own order, Jamaica said, "Let me know when you want that lesson." She waved at an employee calling to her from the sales counter. "Got to go. Enjoy your breakfast. I'll see you tonight." She gave Caroline's shoulder a squeeze before heading to the kitchen.

Caroline's time at the bank went easy enough. Michael had told her which documents she would likely need to open an account. As promised, he'd also provided the check to deposit in the new account. The entire event went smoothly. As she exited the bank, she felt lighter and proud of taking the first big step in managing her own money.

Elowen Sparkle and Caroline hit it off at several Business Women's Alliance meetings. After helping Isabelle make jam at the bakery for a couple of weeks, Caroline gave her notice and joined Elowen at Sparkle Jewelry. During their conversations, the shop owner was impressed with Caroline's knowledge of jewelry and gemstones. With Caroline at the helm in Fulton River, Elowen planned to open a new store in Montpelier. Part of the new store's inventory would be most of Caroline's jewelry on consignment. Elowen offered to set Caroline up as the lead saleswoman in Montpelier. Caroline turned it down, explaining that she wanted to stay in Fulton River. Her life was centering there now, and she didn't want to unsettle it again. Besides, she didn't want to run into her old so-called friends. Not that she was embarrassed to be working. She didn't want to deal with all their questions.

CHAPTER THIRTY-EIGHT

A week before Labor Day, Caroline made dinner for Michael at the condo. He was still living at his parent's house to give Caroline the space and time she needed to solidify her plans.

"That was a terrific dinner, Caroline," Michael said truthfully after polishing off the last of the beef Wellington.

She smiled, looking pleased. "Gina taught me some easy things that look impressive. She's planning to increase my repertoire over the next few months."

Michael smiled and raised his hand. "Happy to be your guinea pig." He could feel his knees jittering under the table. The air was heavy in the room, potent and charged with impending news.

She peered up at him from beneath her eyelashes. "I'm working with Elowen Sparkle now," she announced as she collected the dishes and took them to the sink.

"She's smart to hire you. That's a perfect fit for you," Michael said, joining her at the counter to wash the dishes.

"I've got this," she said, shooing him away.

Ringo jumped up onto Michael's lap when he sat on the sofa. "I see your new cat is doing well." She had surprised him when she asked to adopt Ringo. He'd thought it might remind her of the attack at the house, but both of them seemed happy with the arrangement.

Michael gave the feline the petting he was begging for. "I didn't realize you were eating beef again."

"Minimally." She flashed him a mischievous smile. "Bacon a little more often." Caroline winked as she wiped the last hand-washed dish dry and placed it in the cabinet.

"How come you don't use the dishwasher?" Michael chuckled.

It was Caroline's turn to chuckle. "It's – it's a long story. I'll tell you later." The sound of her mirth warmed his body like a down comforter on a cold Vermont night.

Caroline sat down beside him and angled her body toward him. "I wanted to talk to you about my future."

His shoulders stiffened as she continued, "I've been going to the psychotherapist regularly. It's helping a lot. It helped me see I've created an association between sex and violence that's not healthy. We both know where it stems from."

Michael nodded and remained silent.

"It will take time to change that thinking."

Michael's stomach erupted in butterflies. Did he dare hope she would rule in his favor? She had used the word "my future" instead of "our future" which didn't feel reassuring.

"I've decided to ask you to come live with me. As my best friend, my partner. And the husband you are." She paused, her cheeks beginning to flush, her eyes darting around the room. "If you'll still have me to be your lawfully wedded wife."

She reached out and pulled the prenup contract from the chair beside her. "I had the attorney revise the prenup to remove the no-intimacy clause. Here's a copy for you to review. If you approve of the change, we can make an appointment to make this new version official."

He lunged for her, his heart bursting through his chest wall. The abrupt movement sent Ringo airborne and he scurried out of sight. Michael crushed Caroline to him and covered her face with kisses. "Yes. To all of it." Then he set her aside and began digging into his pants pocket. His fisted hand opened to reveal two rings made of tourmaline stone.

"Will you accept this ring as proof of my love and our marriage?" He held up the smaller ring for her inspection. "It's not the usual wedding ring."

"Oh, but it means so much more than a plain ring of gold or platinum," she said, extending her left hand. "You got that in Bass Harbor, didn't you?"

QUEST FOR LOVE

"I did. I never got a chance to share them with you." Michael slipped the ring on her fourth finger. "Are you sure it won't bring up bad memories?"

"Memories about the time you helped save my life? Or about falling in love with you on Mount Desert Island? Let me do yours." She took the remaining ring and slid it on his ring finger.

"It's official now. We can tell the world?" Michael said.

"Yes, until death do us part."

Acknowledgements

Hillary Clinton once said it takes a village to raise a child. The same is true to turn a blank page into a novel. My lovely village is small, and selective. It starts with my critique partner, Valerie Lynne. We meet nearly every month, either by Zoom or in the Warwick, Rhode Island Panera for our power hours. We are also good friends! How could we not be as we share our stories and the struggles we face trying to write while fulfilling our routine life tasks. Valerie's support is crucial to my progress and I thank you, Valerie, for being with me on my journey. Your support means the world to me. (If you haven't read Valerie's books, you are truly missing some great reads! See her website for more information at valerielynnebooks.com)

This book would be a disaster without my diligent beta-readers, Marion and Patti. These ladies read the early manuscript and tell me everything that's wrong with it. And I love them for their honesty and hard work.

Lastly, my editor, Lynne Hancock Pearson at All That Editing, LLC. Your attention to detail and constructive comments never fail to point me to those pesky plot holes and inconsistencies. You are the best and I'd be lost without your guidance. I can't thank you enough.

Coming this Fall!

Title to be announced
Colby County Series: Book Three

That cute groomsman is crooking his finger. Is he looking at me? Tulsi Anthony glanced around her. There was no one except Cortland in the immediate vicinity. *Couldn't be for me,* she thought as determinedly as she could. He is good looking with a slim but sturdy body. Flashes of what he might look like naked piqued her interest. *If I head to the bar, maybe he'll meet me there?* "I think I need another sea breeze," Tulsi muttered to Cortland.

She chewed on the end of her swizzle stick with her eyes on Cortland Stewart. Cortland wasn't drunk. She was swiveling her head around to keep eye on her former boyfriend who was somewhere in the event hall. Tulsi glanced toward the come-hither guy and spotted Hannah's mother waving from halfway across the room.

Tulsi groaned as the woman started for her, walking a wobbly path. When dark amber liquid sloshed out of drink glass she was holding, Mrs. Woodbridge didn't even notice.

"Dr. Anthony, I was hoping you would be wearing a traditional sari tonight." The woman sat down in the empty seat beside her. "I just love the colors. Indian women's attire is always so —exotic."

Ugh, here we go. Pasting a fake smile on her lips she said, "Your daughter asked me to be a bridesmaid. So I had to wear the dress she picked out for us to wear." It was a true statement. Far better than admitting she didn't own a sari and having to explain. *Why do people always think just because I'm clearly of Indian descent I would automatically have one. And know how to cook curries, or eat dosa or naan and practice yoga every day.*

Mrs. Woodbridge stood, "That's too bad. I'm sure you would have looked beautiful in one." She tottered away heading in the direction of the bar so disjointedly Tulsi hoped the bartender would cut her off, or at the very least, Mr. Woodbridge was driving tonight.

It was nearly midnight, when the festivities would end. Between the BFF bachelorette party last night and the wedding ceremony and reception today, she was exhausted. That didn't include her drive up from Louisiana a little over a week ago. Plus moving in to Cortland's former condo, settling in at the clinic, and, oh yeah, four days of work. *Talk about being thrown into the fire.*

She shook it off, sipping on the swizzle stick like it was a straw. Which it wasn't. She was grateful for having made it to Hannah and Andrew's wedding. Honored to have been asked to serve as a bridesmaid.

A movement caught her eye. That slim, light-haired guy smiled when she met his eyes. She decided to ignore him again, even though he was mighty cute, as in baby-faced cute. A lock of his bangs flopped down onto his forehead rather roguishly. His index finger beckoned again. He couldn't be trying to entice her, could he?

Everyone that was left in the hall had broken up into couples, except for her, Cortland and the groomsman. *Scratch that.* Over Cortland's shoulder she could see him advancing toward her. His index finger crooking as if he was summonsing her to come to him. Heat flushed through her face. His head bobbed to one side and he winked.

Well, well. He is singling me out. This night is looking up. A twinge of sexual attraction made a smile blossom on her face. She lowered her eyes in a flirtatious manner, not yet willing to give in to his luring antics.

Cortland must have noticed her blushing. She turned around and caught sight of him. "I think Lucas wants to dance with you." She leaned forward and whispered in Tulsi's ear, "Go get'm, cowgirl." Then she gave her a wink.

Lucas. The other firefighter in the wedding party besides Dawson. Tulsi gulped down the last of her drink. "I'm going to get another. Do you want anything?"

"He's kind of messed up."

That was not what she'd expected and shock of it must have shown.

Lucas swiftly continued, "His ankle is healing fine, but his heart...not so much."

"She's really bummed he refused to going with her to Alaska."

Lucas pulled her closer. So close she could feel his erection pressing against her lower abdomen. "Let's not talk about them," he whispered. "Let's talk about the remainder of our night."

QUEST FOR LOVE

At Cortland's ear to ear grin, Tulsi set down the empty glass and stood. Locking eyes with him, she jerked her head toward the bar. Lucas Campbell, a firefighter with the Colby Fire Department grinned and moved to intercept her.

"Having a good time tonight?" He asked as he handed his empty beer bottle to the bartender. "Another please. And anything this beauty wants."

"Sea Breeze." Tulsi said. "Yes, it's been fun. And great to see my girlfriends again. I've missed them."

His nod brought that loose lock of hair flopping down onto his forehead. "You're the new veterinarian at the Colby clinic?"

She raised her eyebrows. "That's me. I'm replacing Cortland."

"I heard you three were tight in college."

"Vet school, yeah. It feels good to be back on the east coast."

A quizzical expression erupted on his face. "Where were you?"

"Small community in rural Louisiana. And glad to be back here."

"That bad?"

"The stories I could tell." She held up her palm as if swearing on a bible. "Every one of them true."

The tired looking bartender slid their fresh beverages across the countertop. "Eighteen."

Lucas handed the guy a twenty dollar bill. "Keep the change."

They walked away from the bar stand, to a cocktail table in an area beside the dance floor. Tulsi sipped at her drink. This was only her third Sea-Breeze but she'd had two glasses of wine during dinner. She hadn't anticipated finding a man so she hadn't held herself in check. Like Cortland, she planned to call an Uber to get home.

She eyed Lucas over her drink. He was definitely handsome. His body might be filled out in the manly manner, but his baby face made him look like he should still be in high school. There was also something in it that gave Tulsi the impression he was not quite one hundred percent Anglo Saxon white male. Perhaps it was the darkness of his eyes, nearly black. And his skin looked tanned, like permanently tanned. *If I play my cards right, I can get him naked and find out if it's skin tone or tan.* She smiled rather than sip at her tiny cocktail straw.

"What's so funny?" He asked, leaning into her ear. His breath tickled her lobe, making her lady parts jolt awake.

The dance music was a little rowdy. There wasn't much time left before the DJ and the venue shut down for the night. Tulsi wondered if he was going to ask her to go home with him. *Scratch that. It's the twenty-first century. I'll ask him.* "I was just thinking about going home. With you."

Lucas' eyes bugged wide at first, then glistened with amusement. "Tell me more. What do you think would happen?"

She raised an eyebrow in a way she hoped was flirtatious. "I think we would end up in my bed."

Lucas visibly gulped. "To sleep?" His eyes searched hers with a look of bridled glee.

Tulsi smiled over her drink again with a sparkle in her eyes. She slowly shook her head.

His smile blossomed before gulping down more beer.

Tulsi was sure if he couldn't believe his ears. She gnawed on her fresh swizzle stick. *Being a cougar is kind of fun.* "That is if you want to come home with me. In an Uber, of course."

He jerked his head toward the dance floor.. "Let's dance."

She hadn't been paying much attention to the music during their conversation. A slow dance was playing. As they headed out to the dance floor, she spied Dawson surprising Cortland at their banquet table.

On the dance floor, Lucas drew her close against his body. He swayed in place a few moments before pulling her into the dance. The man knew how to lead. It was her turn to feel terrified. She blurted the first thing she could think of. "How's Dawson feeling?" She jerked her head toward Dawson and Cortland.

Don't miss out!

Visit the website below and you can sign up to receive emails whenever Diana Rock publishes a new book. There's no charge and no obligation.

https://books2read.com/r/B-A-YUKN-RQMTC

BOOKS 2 READ

Connecting independent readers to independent writers.

Also by Diana Rock

Colby County Series
Bid To Love
Courting Choices

Fulton River Falls
Melt My Heart
Proof of Love
Bloomin' In Love
First Christmas Ornament: A Fulton River Falls Novella
Quest For Love

MovieStuds
Hollywood Hotshot

Standalone
Little Bit of Wait
Havilland's Highland Destiny: A Contemporary Highland Romance

Watch for more at DianaRock.com.

About the Author

Diana lives in eastern Connecticut with her tall, dark and handsome hero and two mischievous felines. She works full time as a histotechnologist, writing in her spare time. Diana likes puttering about the yard, baking and cooking, hiking, fly-fishing, and Scottish Country Dancing. Sign up for Diana's newsletter at DianaRock.com to receive special news, and free bonus material.

Read more at DianaRock.com.